THE PARIS SYNDROME

Other published works by John Roman Baker

Novels
No Fixed Ground
The Dark Antagonist
The Sea and the City

Plays
The Crying Celibate Tears Trilogy

Poetry
Cast Down
The Deserted Shore
Gethsemane
Poèmes à Tristan

THE PARIS SYNDROME

John Roman Baker

WILKINSON HOUSE

FIRST EDITION
Wilkinson House Ltd
November 2012

ISBN 978-1-899713-30-1

Wilkinson House Ltd.,
145-157 St. John Street,
London, EC1V 4PW
United Kingdom

www.wilkinsonhouse.com
info@wilkinsonhouse.com

Cover design: R. Evan / M. Sanchez
Cover photos: © Alexey Utemov / iStock Photo / R. Evan

British Library Cataloguing-in-Publication Data
A catalogue record for this book is available from the British
Library.

for Colston

Paris syndrome (French: *Syndrome de Paris*) is a transient psychological disorder encountered by some individuals visiting or vacationing in Paris, France. It's characterised by a number of psychiatric symptoms such as acute delusional states, hallucinations, feelings of persecution (perceptions of being a victim of prejudice, aggression or hostility from others), derealisation, depersonalisation, anxiety, and also psychosomatic manifestations such as dizziness, tachycardia, sweating and others.

Part One
The North

I have two sons. One is dark, one is fair and yet I cannot decide which is the darker. I look at the fair youth and see darkness; I look at the dark youth and see a brilliant light. Another day I might look at the fair one and he is fair and the dark one dark. I hurry to the fair for comfort, and to the dark for some knowledge of the night. I have two sons, and both bring me a sense of hope, and with that hope an equal amount of despair.

I called the fair boy Francis when he was born. I chose that name because of my passion for St. Francis of Assisi. This boy will be good, I told myself, and I wanted so much for him to be good. I wanted him to save me from the dark fears I had within me. When, less than a year later, my second son was born, I called him Thomas, after Thomas in the gospels who doubted. The first time I held him in my arms he felt heavy, and I sensed a fear in myself that I would love him less than Francis.

My wife died soon after Thomas's birth. Her death was quite sudden. I woke one morning to find she was dead in our bed. A heart attack, the doctor said. I blame myself for sleeping too heavily the night she died. Had she a moment of awareness, a need to share before her death, that my deep sleep denied her? I have told myself the brutal suddenness of the attack would have obliterated all need to share, but a part of me has remained unsure and consequently guilty. Since that night I have not slept heavily again and find that I wake up every half hour, vividly alert to the silence around me and the darkness of the room, as if I have become a sentinel waiting for a call.

"Father."

I heard the call.

Two years after the beginning of this fractured sleep I was awakened by the call of Thomas. The housekeeper generally looked after the boys, but no one heard him except me. I ran to his room, and he was sitting up in bed shaking. When I took him in my arms he clung to me and said he had seen terrible things. When I asked him to explain he said that he could not; that the dark was too dark, despite the small nightlight in his room and the aura of light that it gave. I turned on a brighter light and told him a story. I chose the brightest and sunniest story I could, but everything I did that night to ease his panic and his fear failed. When at last I returned to my room I felt I would never have an opportunity to comfort this dark boy, and the thought filled me with a sense of failure.

Years passed. I was a young man when they were born, in those brief years when I was having sexual intercourse with my wife. In the ten years that followed her death I did not seek out anyone to replace her. I wished to return to the homosexual life I had before I met her; before I had been consumed by the desire to bring sons into the world, and the accomplishment of that desire through her. After her death I admitted to myself that I had not loved her, that I had in fact used her.

As those years passed I suffered a great deal from the guilt of knowing that I had used her body solely in the hope that it would bring me sons. I had thanked God while she was alive for granting my wish, but when she was dead I realised that thanks to any God were bitter deceptions. Before I met her I did not believe in God, so along with my use of her body I had used a fictitious God to give thanks to. Maybe with her living presence (those brief years of meeting her and her pregnancies and then her death) I had wanted a God to stabilise me, to secure me as it were against the revelation of my own cynicism in using her. But then with her absence and the presence of the two boys I faced up to the truth about myself.

"Father."

It was Thomas again. Ten years old and staring at me with big, dark brown eyes.

"Yes," I said.

"Father, why are you so alone?"

I smiled at him and then I looked at Francis who was standing behind him. Francis was eleven then, but looked older. Why had he not noticed I was alone? Why was it the dark one who was able to tell me this and not him? I knew I had wanted Francis to speak these words, but he had remained silent. I even wanted to ask him what he thought, but I remained silent.

"Father, why don't you reply?"

I smiled again and walked away. Behind me I heard a stifled sob. I felt I had dealt a first blow against my dark son.

After this, I kept myself away from them as much as possible. Isabelle, the housekeeper, took care of them, and I locked myself away. I would not even have meals with them. No more questions were asked and they began to grow up. Occasionally, I would leave the house and go to places for anonymous sex with other men. The sex gave me little pleasure, and I found I got more satisfaction being with my books than with other people. I was studying the Italian Renaissance and writing a book about it. In fact I was adding nothing much to what had already been written, but I refused, while I was in the act of writing, to admit that this too was a failure. Only when the book was finished did my thoughts focus again upon my sons.

It was a day in mid-August.

I saw my sons frequently, but all the time I had been occupied with my book and my unsatisfying sexual encounters I had not really looked at them. I had deliberately not acknowledged they were on the brink of manhood. It took my housekeeper to point out, on that day in mid-August, that they were becoming restless and hard to handle.

"What is the problem?"

She stared back and shook her head.

"They have passed all their exams. School is finished. You know this already. We talked about it."

"Oh," I replied.

She shook her head again, and I could see she was repressing her anger.

"It is as if you hate any knowledge of them," she said abruptly.

I felt a coldness go through me. The room was hot and quite suddenly I was cold.

"That's not true," I replied.

"Isn't it?"

She looked at me, a look of challenge in her eyes.

"They have time on their hands now," she added. "They need to do something different. While you were writing your book they were studying. Now you have finished your book, and they have finished their studies. It is time to move on."

"Move on to where?"

I looked blankly at her. Did she mean it was time for us to leave this house: this house that had been in my family for generations, and move away? If that was what she meant, I had no intention of doing so. I think she saw my confusion and clarified herself.

"Francis and Thomas need to go away. They need to spend a few months travelling. You know as well as I do, they know nothing besides this house and the schools they have been to."

She was right of course, and I said I would speak with my sons and ask them what they wanted.

I saw both of them together. I was surprised at how they had grown and what handsome youths they had become. I looked at Francis for a long while, absorbed in his fair beauty. I realised I desired my son.

"Francis," I asked, "is it true you would like to travel?"

He nodded his head.

"I think you know that," he said. "I want to go to France."

I turned to Thomas. His eyes were darker than I remembered, but they flashed brightly in the bright afternoon of the August day.

"And you? Where would you like to go, Thomas?"

"Spain," he said simply.

"Where in Spain?"

"Barcelona."

"Why to Barcelona?"

"I want to discover another culture. I know I'll find something I want in Spain, and especially in Barcelona."

I agreed to their journeys. I asked no more questions that afternoon, but in my bed that night I dreamt that Francis would be in trouble if I did not give him some advice. The advice I had to give was so simple and yet so obscure I felt foolish in approaching him. All the same, the next day I had a meeting with him. Thomas was there also.

"Francis," I said, "I want to advise you."

He looked at me and his face was closed to my words. I knew he was completely closed to me. All that light in him and he was excluding me, but I persisted.

"Francis, I want you to travel around France, but take your bicycle. It's a good way to travel at your age."

He gave a short little laugh.

"Please don't laugh at me. I feel it to be right. I have never asked you for anything, but I'm asking you now. I would like you to travel light, with a bicycle and two books by Hemingway."

"I studied *The Old Man and the Sea* at school," he said.

"Did you like it?"

"Yes," he answered.

He smiled at me for the first time. I saw light in his face at last.

"That's good."

"But why is it good, Father?"

I think this was the first time in a long time he had called me Father, and I trembled with desire and love to hear him use that word.

"Because the words are simple," I replied, "and you are a child of light. You will not be harmed by the apparent simplicity of Hemingway, and at the same time you will discover a little more about the world without having to experience its darkness. Hemingway can be a writer of darkness, but the horizontal simplicity of the narratives will protect you. A bicycle and two books by him. That is all you need for your trip to France."

"Can you suggest two titles?" he asked.

There was the slightest tone of sarcasm in his voice, but he smiled at the same time, and I brushed the thought aside. I wanted to hold him, to hug him, but I could not infect him with the physical contact of my body. My dream had spoken. My inner self had spoken. It was not my daily, living flesh, but my night dream self that had produced this knowledge. He was protected from the real me by that.

"*A Farewell to Arms* and *The Sun Also Rises*."

"Thank you, Father."

Immediately after he had thanked me, Thomas spoke up. His voice was deeper than that of Francis, and I noticed a surly expression on his face. He looked like a lover who had been rebuffed. It was a look of hatred.

"You do not need to advise me," he said. "I know exactly what you will tell me."

"How do you know that, Thomas?" I asked. I did not tell him I had no intention of advising him at all.

"Because I know you, Father."

These words made me shudder. I wished suddenly he had never been born. I realised he was the very centre of darkness for me, and that I was afraid of him. In my mind the thought cried out, please, please Francis, rescue me.

"I need no advice on what I shall take or how I should

travel," he continued. "I have chosen to go by train to Barcelona, and I will buy my own books there. You see, Father, I love books far more than Francis, and I know they are to be my life. I need no protection from any reading or any mode of travel."

"You're right," I said without looking at him. "That is exactly how I would have advised you."

I left them and went to my room. I wanted to sleep. I suddenly needed to sleep and not dream, but even as I closed my eyes I felt the shadows move in on me, the hidden invaders who crept into my mind, making images and speaking with many voices. I forced sleep away, not wanting it, and got out of bed. I sat at my work table and read through the book I had written, the book of all those years I had not been with my sons. I read the words I had written and it all seemed hopelessly useless and trivial. I repeated to myself again that it had all been written out so many times before me, and probably better. I shut the book and threw it down on the floor. I paced the room until the house was quiet, until everyone was in their beds. I opened my door and made my way to Francis's room. I stood outside and saw a light beneath his door. Raising my hand, I knocked lightly.

"Who is it?"

His clear voice behind the door sounded cautious, almost afraid.

"Your father."

"Come in, Father."

I opened the door and went into his room. This was his sanctuary, and I had never invaded it. Had I been in it before? Of course I must have, but I no longer remembered. I saw how neat everything was. On the walls he had a few posters. The usual posters adolescent boys have of footballers and topical celebrities. Beneath the posters, an empty bookshelf with a small globe of the world on one of the shelves; next to the globe, two small silver statues of football players. There was not one book to be seen. The bed was folded back, and he was standing by the bed, naked from the waist upwards. I stared at his white chest and at his two brown nipples. I wanted to reach out and touch him. At that moment I knew I should have watched him grow up, that this should not be such a surprise. His body should have been familiar to me, but it was not. He was as unfamiliar to me as any man or boy I had had occasional sex with, but he was more desired, and that I had to admit, fully and totally. I could not hide the truth from myself, even if I was never, ever to let him know what I felt.

"What do you want, Father?"

He was looking at me coldly now. There was no smile on his face. Would I ever be able to make him smile again?

"I was passing, and I saw your light under the door. I was on my way down to the library. I have the two Hemingways, and I thought I would get them for you."

"It could have waited."

He lowered his trousers as he said this. He was totally unconscious of the effect this was having on me. He had absolutely no idea he was an object of desire. I was just another man like himself and not to be hidden from. He turned his back as he slid down his underwear, and I looked quickly at his buttocks, even whiter than the rest of his body. I longed for him to turn and face me, but he got into bed, and within a second his body was covered.

"You're not really going to get them for me tonight, are you?"

He looked at me from his bed and putting a hand to his face, yawned.

"No, it can wait until morning. After all, you're not going tomorrow, are you?"

He laughed and snuggled down.

"I think I will go as soon as I can. Thomas and I don't have to leave together. After all, we are not going to the same place."

"But you are going part of the same distance," I replied.

"Thomas has his life. I have mine."

The words were said with a sort of finality.

"But you do love your brother?" I asked.

"Love?" he questioned.

He looked at me with his cold blue eyes.

"I'm not sure I love him exactly, but I get on with him."

"I have been so –" I paused.

"Yes, Father?"

"Distant. I have been working on my book. Not looking properly at either of you."

"We have all had work to do," he murmured, his voice beginning to sound tired. "It's normal we didn't see you while you had all that work. We were told how important it was for you to complete it, and we accepted it. At least I did."

"And Thomas? How did he feel about my distance?"

"We never talked about you," he said.

"What did you talk about?"

It was as if the floodgates had opened, and suddenly I needed to know things I should have asked about long before.

"Father, would you put out the light? I really am tired. All I can say to your question is that we were distant with each other, Thomas and I. Friendly, but distant."

He looked at me, and I caught a look of recrimination in his eyes. He added quietly, "After all we never grew up with a woman in the house. Men don't really have much open feelings for each other, do they?"

I could not answer him. His look was too piercing. I felt I had to leave the room. Before going I did as he asked and turned off the light. He said thank you and I replied goodnight, leaving the room and closing the door behind me. As I came out onto the landing, Thomas came towards me. He was dressed and looked as if he was going to Francis's room.

"Hello," he said.

I smiled at him and said I had just had a talk with Francis. He looked at me in surprise as I said this and then laughed loudly. I asked him to be quiet as I did not want Francis to hear him.

"We don't see you to talk to for years," he said, "and now you visit one of our rooms. Were you coming to mine after his?"

"No."

"I thought not."

"Shall we talk downstairs?" I asked.

He shrugged.

"If you were not coming to talk to me, why do we have to talk at all?"

"Francis is thinking of leaving soon. Do you have the same intention?"

He did not reply to this but moved away towards the stairs. I followed him down to the living room. A fire was still burning in the grate. On a small table there was an open book. He caught my eye as I looked at the book and saw he had been reading.

"May I see?" I asked.

He picked up the book and handed it to me. It was a volume of Georg Trakl's poems in German.

"There was a word in *Grodek* I did not understand. I was going to get the German dictionary on the landing. I lost mine and haven't replaced it yet. You knew I'd been studying German at school, didn't you?" he asked simply. "Or perhaps you didn't follow my courses closely enough to know that."

"I also did German at school," I replied, and looked at the poem. "What is the word?"

He shook his head at me and took the volume from my hands.

"It's late. Enough German for tonight. I will look the word up in the morning."

"Do you trust a dictionary better than me?" I asked.

He laughed again. It was a softer laugh now. Not harsh or ugly like the laughs so many people have, but almost a caress. A beautiful laugh. Totally unlike the laugh I had heard from him on the landing.

"Sit down, Father. Have a drink."

He went and poured me a whisky.

"Do you drink?" I asked.

"Yes," he said. "I like one drink when I am studying. It warms me to every subject. You don't mind, do you?"

"No."

"Good."

He poured himself a similar amount to mine.

"We probably won't see much of each other before I go on this trip, so let's have a drink on it."

Unlike with Francis, I had no impression of talking to an adolescent youth. He seemed as old as I was. Even his voice was deeper than mine, and deeper than his brother's. I also recognised it was a more pleasant voice than his brother's. At least, that is how it seemed in the situation we were in. I took the drink from him and we clinked glasses.

"Cheers," I said.

"Cheers, Father."

We sat and faced each other across the fire. The last time I had done this was with his mother. That was now all so far in the past, and I had no desire to speak about her to either of my sons. Why? Guilt again? Indifference? A mixture of both? She had provided me with what I desired, and yes, I really did feel guilt that I felt desire towards one of the human gifts she had given me. I drank my whisky quickly and went to pour another.

"Father, you are a disturbed man."

He said this slowly. I turned and stared at him.

"Why are you a disturbed man?"

"Really, I –"

My voice trailed off. I felt trapped with him.

"Is it because you have never felt love for any of us?" he asked.

"I have loved all of you."

"My mother too?"

He stared hard at me. This was no youth in front of me, but

an interrogating old man. Thomas was old, so old, and I knew in my heart, and dare I say it in my soul, that he had travelled in some mysterious way through centuries of living. I felt suddenly like a child in front of him.

"Your mother too."

I said this flatly. I didn't care if he understood I was not being truthful with him. He got up, poured himself another drink, and I saw an old drunk in front of me. All I could think of was: the old man is pouring himself more to drink, and there is nothing I can do to stop him. He needs to drink. I noticed his glass was fuller than it had been before.

"I don't drink it with soda either," I said stupidly. I had nothing left to say. He raised his drink to toast me. For what reason, I didn't ask. The situation, if there was a situation, was out of my control. It was lost to me because unlike Francis I wanted nothing of Thomas, and certainly had no desire to impose my will over him. He could drink all he liked.

"Why did you give him Hemingway?"

The question disturbed me. I shrugged. It had been in my dream to do so, that's all, but how could I tell him anything so seemingly ridiculous? Who and what after all was Hemingway to me? I had seen film versions of his novels and had liked them. I had read *A Farewell to Arms* and been moved by its love story. It's true I had been an adolescent myself when I had done so, and when in later years I had re-read the book I found there was a hollowness at its core I had not felt before. The woman had not seemed real the second time around, but then again in my actual life no woman around me appeared real, including my recently married wife. They shared the same name though, Catherine. I had observed that. The unreal, ideal woman from the book and my wife had the same name. Other than that I had read a few of his short stories, but despite my liking for *The Sun Also Rises* I had not read the book, relying almost entirely on the film. I was aware, as a writer, that Hemingway's style had been influential on many for its apparent simplicity, and for leaving out a lot the reader could divine for his or herself. Hemingway often used the metaphor of the iceberg, with only the tip being seen and written about. The rest left below the surface. Like my feelings for my own dead Catherine and for my sons. I realised I had ignored his question by staring into a darkened corner of the room.

"Why Hemingway for Francis?" Thomas repeated.

"It was intuition," I answered. It was the nearest I wanted to go into my dream world with him, but I did ask him if he had read Hemingway himself.

"*Men Without Women.*" He said the title with an edge of sarcasm. "Bullfighters and hard drinkers. Masculine, rough men. Killers too." He paused. "Is that the world you want to give my brother to read about? Francis seems pretty clear cut to me. He's not an adventurer. Not really. In fact, I think he wants the opposite of the masculine world."

"I offered him two novels that are not like those stories," I replied, suddenly defensive.

"Not *The Sun Also Rises*?" he replied. "The macho world of man and bull. I am surprised you did not offer it to me. Most of it is focused on Spain. Paris too, but his heart was in Spain."

"You had no desire for me to offer you any book," I replied, driven into the beginnings of an argument.

"Did your intuition tell you I had no need of your help?"

"Yes," I said, as sharply as I could.

"You were right in that I can choose for myself, but wasn't part of the reason your simple indifference towards me?"

We looked at each other in silence. I held his look, confused and in a way overwhelmed by the darkness I felt between us. We looked, but we were strangers, and it seemed to me we would never be anything else.

"I am tired," I said at last.

He laughed again and drank the whisky down in one go.

"Time to go to bed then," he said.

I did not reply. I stared in silence at the fire.

"It's over-hot in here. A fire in August. Is it necessary?"

"English summers," he murmured, poking at the coals. "I won't need a fire in Spain. I will be glad to be there."

"Good," I replied, and standing, made my way to the door.

"Father."

His voice chilled me. Please let me go, I begged, without saying the words. It is too hot in here with you. I had my back to him, but I turned again and faced him.

"Thank you," he said.

"For what?"

"I'm not as old as you think I am."

Had he read my thoughts? I tried again to see a youth, an inexperienced youth sitting there, and I stared hard at him as if somehow I wanted to find him, but I could not.

"Why should I think that," I replied, hiding myself like the squid that sends out its protective shield. I wanted to slip away into the dark waters.

"I know with my mind," he said slowly.

It was as if he would never really communicate with me, never really get to some part of me that could matter to both of us. But I still wanted to remain in hiding and needed to get out of the room and his presence.

"You have a very fine, abstract mind," I said. My voice sounded neutral and distant even to me.

"I have no experience," he added.

He was staring at the flames in the fire and not at me. I felt a sudden impulse to go to him, but repressed it immediately. I crushed within myself any desire to make real contact with Thomas. To me it felt like an obscenity to have even the slightest desire to approach him. After all, what would I do? Touch his shoulder? Put an arm around him? His voice was plaintive and needy, and I needed Francis, who was as I saw it totally oblivious to me. It was stalemate all the way around.

"Experience will come," I said curtly, and then I left the room. I thought I heard a cry as if someone had been hit, but as I walked away from the door I realised that like so much, it was all only in my imagination. Part of me had done the crying out against the curt brutality of my voice's expression. I had refused the possible real need of my son, and I returned to my room, ashamed at my sense of failure.

That night my dream world attacked me with a ferocity I had never experienced before. Just before going to sleep I had turned on the radio and listened to the end of Cherubini's *Requiem in C minor*. The beautiful music wove its way into my mind, and between the sounds I heard were the words:

You are alone, you are alone, you are completely alone. This music is not to comfort you, but to make you hear the utter uselessness of beauty. To hear how it slides away, mournfully into darkness, in mourning for its own beautiful self – a self that in itself can be an inspiration, but also a death. A requiem. This is the requiem of what has been. For what is to come.

The words I knew came from within myself, yet I had the hallucinatory impression they were coming to me from the radio, from within the music itself, and once the dying sounds had ended, still they continued:

Your wife, where is your wife now, and where was she all the pitiful months you pretended to play such a cold passion upon her body? She is here in the icy space of this music, in the lingering sound of her voice that you never heard, as you refused just a while ago to listen to the cry of your son.

I insisted it was in my imagination, but the torturing words lashed at me, insisting that I had truly heard them and that ultimately it did not matter who had uttered them:

The cry was there, is there, and maybe if you went to his door you would hear him now, calling out a name.

"What name?" I answered in the silence, the brief silence that had ended the music, but the music returned and the lilting sounds of a Vivaldi concerto followed the Cherubini. I turned off the radio and turning onto my left side, closed my eyes. Darkness was darker there in the absence of outer life. I drifted a while into a place that seemed suddenly gentler, a place that was like an inner light and calm as the stone of an ancient, yet enduring city. I swayed there on that sea of light, and then threading out with needles of darkness, the light was overcome, and then gone. I was in a grey land on that borderland of sleep, where the grasp of real sleep at last takes control. No longer myself, and yet totally within, I let go and fell into a melting, dissolving gallery of images. One by one the pictures passed by me. Distortions of Piero della Francesca, with broken statue figures and a madness of architecture. This was followed by an obscene Venus emerging from the waves, her hair not hair but the limbs of handsome youths kicking around her head. Towards the darkness of her scalp I could see a writhing tangle of penises, dripping white. The white fell onto her face and then onto her body, sliding down to the sea shell upon which she was standing and beneath that to the sea. The nightmare of her cries blended with my own, and as her image paused, a cruel David emerged from the shadows of this horrible gallery with a knife. He was the same as Michelangelo's *David,* but the hollow white of his eyes was now black, a black of such depth that I was sucked towards it as to a whirlpool. Both eyes merged into one great eye. I felt the coldness of the knife slice into me, and I knew I was dying at last, falling into that final deathly place.

"David," I screamed.

I struggled from my bed. I was overwhelmed by giddiness. I needed to get to the bathroom. The room was revolving dizzily around me, and I tried to clutch onto the nearest object to steady me, but found none. I was dead, wasn't I? The mocking words entered my head and fleetingly I saw the statue of David become a statue of my son Francis. Even in this extremity of fear, desire took hold of me. Francis took the place of the clichéd statue of David. His white buttocks were like a light just beyond my reach, just beyond giddiness, and I reached out for them. If there was no thing to hold onto, couldn't I hold onto them? I stumbled, and then laughter broke the panic and the fear. I heard my own voice laughing at the absurdity of this vision. Was this then the only light possible, this glimpse of flesh, not flesh at all but marble stone? Was this replacement of David to be my way out of fear? His buttocks? My son Francis's buttocks? Was this the reason why I had written my trite book, put words to paper, evoking a past civilisation to justify my stifled desire? The laughter put me on firmer ground. I could stand at last. I was steady on my feet. I opened the door and went to the bathroom.

As I splashed water onto my face the image of Venus returned, and in a brief moment she joined with David. They were there in that moment when the water ran down my face, united in a marriage that suddenly made me think of my own. But as the towel I was reaching for touched my flesh they disappeared into darkness. The mad gallery of the mind had finally departed, and with an unsteady hand I opened the medicine cupboard. I needed diazepam to calm my nerves. I needed to know that when I returned to my bed I would have some assurance of peace. I cupped my right hand for water and downed the pill. Returning to my room, I fell into bed and into a semblance of peace, even if it was not truly peace itself.

The following morning I woke late. I made my way downstairs and heard the voices of Francis and Thomas in the kitchen. They were speaking loudly and did not hear me coming. I stepped to one side of the kitchen door, out of sight, to hear what they were saying.

"I disagree," I heard Francis saying. "It's the first time he's taken an interest. He normally leaves everything to Isabelle, anyone except him. Anyway, I'm tired of talking about him."

"It seems to me he's troubled by something. I'm not sure what."

Thomas's voice was less abrasive, more soothing on the ear, but it was Francis's voice that I wanted to hear, that I liked the sound of.

"His health. He doesn't look well. Look at him closely under a bright light. He looks thin and haggard."

"It's not just that –"

"What then?"

"Something inside him, beyond health. An inner something."

Francis laughed.

"You and your deep stuff. In many ways you remind me of him. All the reading you do. The books you've said you have read, and you always did get higher marks than me."

"Maybe that's because you're not much interested in studying. Rather be out there kicking a football."

Francis made a scoffing sound.

"I know I've got a fitter body than you. You take after him. A bit stringy. Good-looking but stringy. That's what Helena says about you."

I wanted to know who Helena was. By the sound of Francis's voice I sensed intimacy; a girl who was close to one or both of them. I sensed it was probably Francis and she was simply making an observation about Thomas.

"Helena? What does she know? She's only met me twice. She's always with you."

Now I knew. Helena was a close companion of Francis. I felt jealous. I wanted to know what she thought, how she looked, why he was interested in being with her. I knew I had left it too late to get close enough to ask Francis these questions.

"Anyway, I'm tired of being told I'm an idiot. Look at the way he made up that dream or whatever it was about France. Only a month ago I met him, and we talked, and I said I would like to go to Paris. He didn't dream anything. And why does he have to be so mysterious? It's not appealing. He behaves like some fucking clairvoyant, and I'm supposed to go along with it."

"You did. You smiled all the way, even agreeing to the bicycle."

"I'd like to cycle around France. It's true. Got a good bike. But not in Paris. I want to walk in Paris, look at it, take in the people. It's alright for you. You pre-empted him and played along by saying you were capable of making your own decisions. That Spain was your choice. You don't get talked down to like I do."

Had it been like that? It's true I had seen him in my dream on his bicycle in France, and he had two books by Hemingway with him. The dream told me the books would be good for him to read. Not only the ease of prose, but the muscle in the prose. Hemingway was muscular. So was Francis. I liked the lines of my son's body. The statue lines that had tortured me the night before in a very different kind of night experience. It troubled me that I could remember no earlier meeting, no conversation about his desire to go to Paris. I, who remembered all of my encounters with him. Did I only remember from the time when desire began? My thoughts distracted me from what they were saying. Several sentences escaped me.

"He hated her. He hated us as children. Farmed us out to others. Always others."

"We wanted for nothing."

"Materially, no."

"Did you want more, Francis?"

Thomas was being direct here. He was asking that question I could never have asked Francis.

"What do you mean, Thomas?"

"Love."

Another scoffing sound, a sound that was full of ridicule.

"What do I know of it? What do you know of it? Who has ever shown us love? Isabelle? As children it's true he would speak to us and also about us – about us even when we were in the room. Is that love, Thomas?"

"I'm asking you if you wanted more from him."

"Yes."

The explosion of that one word almost blew me apart inside. My stomach turned, and at the same time I felt an exuberant dance inside of me. His *yes* meant he had wanted me, had wanted me as a child. At the same time I felt this inner dance of exuberance, I suddenly felt an equal sensation of shame. I had not noticed them as children. I had been immersed in my endless, long volume on the lives and works of people who had been better described by the likes of Vasari and Berenson. I had a fantasy of ancient Greece and light to combat the darkness in my soul when I had written about the ancient world's influence on the Italian Renaissance. I had also immersed myself in the fantasy of the boys and men that the ancients must have known, must have recreated, and beyond the Greek statues and the Roman statues, Donatello's boys, Michelangelo's men and boys and all the others inspired by the male figure. When I saw Francis in his bedroom standing naked with his back to me, I had seen the trim Donatello David, and also the young David of Michelangelo. I had written tired paragraphs of obvious prose to disguise my own lust for boys and unforgivably to scurry blindly away from the death of my wife. Visible and invisible in my ivory tower I had avoided the reality of those around me.

"You won't get to know them any better by listening at doors."

Isabelle brushed past me as she said this and joined the brothers in the kitchen. She had been with us since my wife became pregnant with Francis, but I didn't really know her. My wife had known her, spoken with her a lot, confided in her, or so she said, but despite all the years she had been with us, I cannot say I knew Isabelle at all. She had never liked me. I knew that. My wife had employed her, and after her death she had stayed on to take care of the boys' needs. I paid her monthly, and occasionally we would utter a few words to each other, but as with my sons I shut myself away from her. I did not see her grow older, had not even noticed her age when she first came into the house. I had inherited money and we were comfortable. Catherine too had come from a well-off family. Money was always available and because of that I never had to think about whether I could afford to keep Isabelle on. I knew she was there and paid her, her salary rising yearly, and left all the regularity of the running of the house to her. She made decisions regarding Francis and Thomas when I was not available, and then as I enclosed myself ever more tightly in the seclusion of my study she began not bothering to inform me and made decisions directly. I let her do it. I let her handle my sons, and I let her handle the household bills. I didn't mind not communicating with her, and in fact the feeling was mutual. When we did speak she would look at me with a sort of contempt and pity that was not hard to interpret. No doubt certain confidences while Catherine had been alive had not endeared me to her. I know Catherine complained about me to her as she had told me so on those rare occasions when we were close enough to each other to argue. "Isabelle knows," she would say enigmatically, but what Isabelle knew exactly she never became explicit about, and I did not care deeply enough to ask. However, judging by her looks of contempt, and the barricade of her unsmiling face, she clearly had no desire for closeness with me. And yet towards the boys she was full of devotion. Between meals and in passing I saw she was a person they related to, and maybe in their way loved. I never asked, and they never mentioned Isabelle when I was with them. So it had been for years, and now she was ready to pass comment as I hid behind the door, listening to my sons. She muttered the words loudly enough for me to hear them, but not for them to be heard by the boys in the kitchen. I turned immediately away and went back the way I had come. I felt the contempt in her words only faintly. I was too profoundly touched by the word *yes* I had heard Francis say, and resentful that she had interrupted me from hearing more.

This is all written down. It has to be written down. In no way is it a journal of what has happened, and is happening, but a sort of recreation in my mind of events. It is not written to know myself any better, but there is on some level a need to examine my passions, my disorientation. I cannot ever know myself, and I do not believe anyone can honestly say they can. I am a mixture of contradictions and phobias, of meditations and impulsive reactions. I can say I know what is happening, but not really why. I am in control when I write down the words here, but that is an illusion that masks the lack of control I have in my own life and over the lives of others. Even though I write thoughts, words and events on these pages to give the impression of control, I sometimes do not believe I have any. Yes, I made a decision to marry, and with the consent of a partner went through with it. Yes, I had two sons by her, but as written here had no deep connection with her. In truth, it was no deeper than a relationship two people might have texting each other. Message sent, message replied. I covered her body with mixed and confused messages, and in return she gave birth to two boys whom I avoided by shutting myself away to write what I see as a useless book. I was in control of all this, or was I? I went through the motions of sexuality like a machine writing ambivalent messages. That is quite simply the history of my relationship with my wife.

I was in control when I shut the door of my study even more firmly after her death than when she was alive. I was in control when I had only the most rudimentary conversations with my growing sons. I was in control when I had occasional meals with them, in control enough not to be bothered by their silence, or alienated by their habitual glancing at their mobile phones for messages between every other mouthful. I in my world, they in theirs. I am in control when I reject mobile phones, texting and all the paraphernalia of early twenty-first century life. To make this easier for me to write, and possibly later on in life to understand, I leave out the gaps where the trivia of computers annihilates narrative. I am not telling the truth by avoiding the endless time wasted, waiting for text messages (especially later on when I came to Paris), for as a writer I see that part of narrative writing as being dead. I am and was sufficiently in control to lie, to heighten tension. I am in control enough, and was in control enough, to both hide and exaggerate my madness. This section is a pause in itself so I can get myself ready to move on to the second section of what happened, or should I say to convey something of what I believe happened. It is a continuing madness, and that word does not make me afraid because I know, old fashioned though the word may sound, that it is an exact word for my state. I do not know myself enough to say in all simplicity (how complex simplicity is) that I am mad, that I was mad and have perhaps always been mad. One example of what I have written up until now shows this to me: the absurdity of telling Francis to travel with two Hemingways and a bicycle. It was in a dream. The dreaming was a revelation and a sort of order. I wanted to order my desired son to do as my dream said he should do – my madness addressing the cold morning of his supposed logic, knowing, in this unknowing of myself, that it was and is physical desire driving me, the desire to open the closed white buttocks of my son, to open him up to me in a way that my nightmare was incapable of doing. I want to see his flesh part. I want to see the tight, rose-coloured muscle appear. I want to widen the tight folds caressed into each other and to immerse myself into that red tunnel, which of course I know leads to darkness. I want to light my way there and to refuse the darkness, to hope that my madness will be able to see me through this impossibility. The writing of this text is the confusion of this desire and the embodiment in words of the terror I feel towards my own yearning. I plunge my pen at the page as I would plunge at his opened body, and the madness of my desire is here in the act of writing. No tapping on a computer keyboard with two hands, but a more physical direction of my will, by using pen on paper in wilful desecration of the pure white, in a splurge and frantic mess of words.

Francis.

I could plunge a thousand times this name upon the page. Francis, Francis, Francis: in the name, the meaning of the text I write, and maybe, if I tried to search, part of the meaning, of what I am myself. Did I plunge into the white body of Catherine, the blonde and beautiful Catherine, so that she could bring out of that plunged place a boy whom I could truly desire? In this pause of narrative I want to let my thoughts run wild, to gallop ahead of me in their obscenity and their intoxication. I can only be drunk with fulfilment in the writing of his name and in the verbal dreaming of the open anus. The anus that in turn becomes his tight closed mouth that seldom smiles at me, that seldom speaks from the heart to me. Except in the word *yes*. I did hear that *yes*, and I did not invent it. There is no exaggeration in it, no embellishment to make the narrative drive forwards. No licence taken. He said the word *yes*, and I felt an uplift of joy.

Thomas.

What a dark shadow across my mind this word produces as I write it. The sleek body, the body of a silken rat. I see him scuttling in the background of my fantasies, and I dread the narrative that is to come, the story that I will write. I dread the fact that the rat will emerge from where it has been hiding and that cornered, I will be at the mercy of its sleek striking body and its painful biting teeth. I dread that I will cover my throat in vain, for I sense its rat's eyes will seek out the opening, and in its own dark desire find the point in which to plunge.

Francis, to my surprise, took his time in leaving. Thomas left before him. I remember I said a few words to Thomas and him to me, but nothing worth recording or remembering. With

Francis it was different. I needed to speak to him, to try to communicate with him before he went on his way. August had reached that time of the month when the light is golden, and while out walking I saw him in the distance, entering a park close to where we had our house. I followed him and found him sitting by a small lake in the middle of the park. He looked bored and a little tired as he sat on a park bench looking out over the water. A group of children were playing around him, and one of them had sent out a boat. I watched him and saw he was taking an interest in this. I approached him. He looked up at me and said as neutrally as possible, "I wanted a boat when I was that lad's age."

"You should have asked."

"Should I?"

A little mocking smile played around his mouth. I noticed how blue his eyes were in the golden day. He moved away as I sat beside him, and I thought, he hates me, he wants to get away from me. A feeling of panic made my hands sweat, and I repeated the words I had first said.

"You should have asked."

He shrugged, said nothing and gazed listlessly out at the boat and the water. The sweat on my hands turned cold. I wiped my hands down the sides of my trousers and felt nothing of the warmth in the air any more.

"When are you leaving?" I mumbled.

He replied he was leaving in a couple of days' time and he was taking the bicycle.

"It needed some repairs," he said. "The gears were risky. In some ways it would have been good to take a flight, but I like boats. I'll be on the water –" he laughed suddenly and pointed out to the toy boat on the lake, "– like that, sailing on an August sea."

He looked like the boy I had rarely seen. He could have been eight or nine years old. His laugh was as high pitched as a child's, and in the gesture of his pointing hand was all the movement of childhood excitement. But as abruptly as he had become a child again the emerging man returned, and the laughter was no longer there. His face aged in a second, and he gazed again at the water and the boat that was now floating rapidly back to the bank. A slight wind had got up, and I looked at his now impassive profile and watched as his hair blew across his face. I wanted to brush it away from his eyes, his fine, fair hair that he liked to have long. I remembered a day many years before, his violent reaction against going to the hairdressers. It was a rare memory I had of him during his childhood. I saw him hit out at the kitchen table, kicking it with his feet, shouting, "No, no, I won't go there. I won't. They are not to touch my hair."

Like the observer I was, and still am in the house, I made no attempt to interfere or reprimand him for his childish rage. As usual I had been between doors, hurrying to get up to my study, or to get out of the door. I saw that last movement vividly as I sat on the bench, yearning to return in time. To be able to stop and go into the room and take him in my arms, and hush his anger with promises or even support him by taking his side and saying, "No, he doesn't have to have his hair cut if he doesn't want to."

I'd had my chance, but like so many others I had been offered I had turned away, barricading my feelings. Or did I in fact feel nothing at all, except the urgency of going to another room or out onto the street: anywhere to escape from the noise of care and responsibility? Instead of a human being in need as he clearly was, I must have seen only my own need: that of my book and the dead images of the Renaissance age I was writing about.

"Francis."

He spoke my name and turned to face me. I had not heard him call me anything else but Father, and wondered for a moment whether it was an illusion of sound in the rising wind. I asked him if he had called me by my name, and instead of replying with a definite yes or no he simply said, "We have the same name, don't we?"

He got up then and automatically I stood up with him. I sensed he wanted to get away from me, that he felt awkward with me and that somehow I was preventing him from leaving.

"You want to rush off, I suppose," I said.

"If that's alright with you. I have things to do."

I wanted to ask what, but kept silent. My hands began to sweat again, and I found it difficult to breathe. There was a note of panic in my voice as I asked again if he had called out my name.

"Francis," he said.

He looked at me, and there was anger in his look. It was obvious he was struggling hard to break away from me, but that I was holding him back. If I had been a stranger, he would have been openly rude and rushed away, but I was still his father and at the very least responsible for his financial needs. I had the power to keep him standing there for as long as I liked, and I had said nothing to release him. In fact, my asking him if he wanted to rush off could have sounded more like a taunt than anything else.

"May I go?"

His suppressed anger made his face red and flushed, or was it the irritation of his hair and the rising force of the wind? He made no attempt with his hands to keep his hair from blowing across his face. Maybe he even wanted the hair to cover his eyes so I would be unable to see what sort of look they had.

"Does it surprise you that we have the same name?" I asked.

A gust of wind blew his hair off his eyes, and the blue glare there was cold. An angry, indifferent coldness, but filled too with frustration and fiercely controlled anger.

"Maybe my mother chose it," he said. His voice was flat and neutral, edged with impatience.

"No, I chose it," I replied.

He shrugged. He made the gesture look as if he was

shrugging off the nervous attacks of the wind. He turned his head and looked out at the lake. Already the wind was making waves, and the boat had bobbed back across the waters, turning away from the green bank and the waiting child who wanted his toy.

"Do you want to know why I chose it?" I insisted.

He continued to look out at the lake, and said nothing. He was trying to detach himself from me by pretending I was not there, that he was alone and free of me. My keeping him prisoner was beginning to excite me. I had him in my power, and I wanted to take full advantage of it.

"When I was your age I played around with the idea of becoming a priest. As a child I had been to Assisi, and I was fascinated by the life of St. Francis. I was a very religious child and went to church regularly. I had no difficulty obeying the wishes of my parents in practising my Catholicism. In fact I am sure they would have been quite pleased if I had told them I wanted to enter the church, and that I was particularly attracted to the Franciscan order."

He remained fixed in place as I talked at him, and as I stared at him I didn't see one muscle move in his body. He looked as if he had been turned to stone.

"Then as the years went by and I reached the age you are now, the desire for entering the church decreased. I am not sure why, but I was still fascinated by St. Francis, and do you know what image fascinated me most about him?"

He made no answer.

"It was the image of Francis discarding his clothes in public, his ability to show the world he could be single, could be alone among them with his own passion for Christ, alone too in his capacity to give up worldly things."

My mind was racing. Was it true what I was saying to him? Had I as a child wanted to enter the church? Had I been fascinated by Francis of Assisi because my religious parents had given me his name, or was it because I had a genuine interest in the man, Francis, and his ability to give up a worldly life? Or was I just using this ploy at this moment in time to keep my son's attention, to keep him there by force, and force this story upon him? I began to feel dizzy. I would have liked to have sat down again, but as I was keeping him there by force, so was I keeping myself by force from moving. It was a vicious circle that despite my excitement was beginning to cause physical discomfort. Francis broke it all by abruptly crying out, "If I don't move away from here and get to a toilet, I am going to piss in my pants. Do you want me to piss in my pants?"

He wheeled on me then, turning his body around, facing me in full anger. He was no longer in control, and his face looked vivid with hatred.

"I have to go."

It was more like a scream. Around us, people were fast leaving the lakeside. The sun was low in the sky, and the wind was becoming a cold wind.

"Alright," I said. "Go."

He ran from me. I watched his body disappear in the retreating crowd of people and slowly I began to retreat myself. For a while I had kept him in my power, but at the end he had defeated me. He had defeated me with the violence of a crude statement. In answer to all my religious sentences he had imposed the image of piss running down his trouser legs. He had killed my lofty words with the image of urine. I realised if he hadn't uttered those words, I would have continued talking at him. There was so much else I had wanted to say. I had wanted to tell him there had been no element of Catholicism or any other religion imposed on him as a child. I had wanted to tell him that unlike my own mother, his mother had not been at all devotional. She was baptised a Catholic, but I had not married her because of that. We had never gone to church, and except for our marriage and for baptisms we had rarely entered one together. God, Christ, the Virgin Mary and the whole panoply of Heaven was foreign to both of us. As soon as I decided to become married

I annulled my relationship with the divine. I had wanted to keep him prisoner there by the lake, reminding him of these things, and he had managed to reject and avoid it all by evoking the image of his urgent need to urinate.

I too needed to relieve myself. The wind and the sudden cold had done its job. I knew of a men's toilet outside the park gates and went there, half hoping to see Francis. Like a game of inner secret chess I wanted to find him there, and there in front of the urinal I would try again to block his move. I would try to imprison him again upon the chess board of my desires, but the toilet was empty except for one stinking old tramp who was standing far back from the bowl, showing off his shrivelled penis. I hurriedly relieved myself and left the place.

For the next few days before he left, Francis managed to avoid me completely. He made sure, despite my attempts to capture him again, that he was not seen. Isabelle had taken herself away to visit relatives, and the house only came alive to the sound of my own steps. I had no need to hurry away from anyone to go to my study. There was no one now to ignore. The barren place was all mine. I did not even hear Francis leave, and when I at last opened the door of his room and entered it again, I found almost all traces of him gone. He had taken down the posters from the walls and put away everything related to his life in the house into cupboards. It was as if he had never lived there. I threw myself down upon his bed, but there was no sense of his body ever having slept there. It had been stripped bare of sheets and bedding, and the only thing that covered it was an old grey counterpane.

"Francis."

I clung to the thin sound of calling his name. It made no impression upon the emptiness of the room, having no reminder of his living there to fall upon. I felt hollow and empty and alone. Then as I got up from his bed I noticed a black sock peeking out from beneath it. I held it up to my face. At last I had a living odour of his flesh. At last there was a remnant of his life in the room, and I breathed it in so hard I thought I would suffocate. Lying on the bed and gloving my right hand with the sock I masturbated to thoughts of his body. I imagined him as St. Francis. I saw him taking off his clothes. In my mind I conjured up people watching him, as excited as I was by his exhibiting himself. As the last article of clothing fell and he stood there in handsome nakedness, I watched as the crowd ejaculated over him. I watched as his nudity was covered with white, dripping slime. He stood as he had stood by the lake, feigning ignorance that he was surrounded at all by others. He ignored the ugly white stains turning to grey water on his body. He ignored the satisfied cries of sexual fulfilment. He stood like the saint that he was, baptised in all of our desires. My hand shook as I peeled off the black glove, stained white. I had defiled the last reminder of his being in the room. I had possessed the last rag of his possessions.

There was no comfort. I went from room to room. I even explored Thomas's room. Contrary to Francis, he had left his place piled high with books and clothes. The sheets were rumpled on his bed, and if I hadn't known he had gone away I would have expected him to re-enter the room at any moment. I had no desire to go through his things and left the room as quickly as I could. I spent the remainder of my time in the house in my study, in the kitchen and in my bedroom. I tried to read, but my mind could not concentrate. In the end I gave in to a depressed apathy and lay for most of the day on my bed, voiding my head as much as possible of all thought. Isabelle found me there on her return from her visit.

"The place is a mess," she said.

"I know," I replied.

"And you don't care?"

"Not much."

"Did you bother to say goodbye to Francis?"

"He didn't bother to say goodbye to me."

"You sound like a petulant child instead of his father."

I wanted to reply that I felt like an abandoned lover, but instead I grinned at her, a silly, ludicrous grin I knew would make her want to leave the room.

"Now you only have to take care of me," I added sarcastically.

"You can do as you have always done."

She spoke to me like an intimate. She spoke to me like a member of the family, and of course in truth, she was. Without her I would not have been able to continue in my sacred solitude all those years. She had been involved in the distant running of my life for so long now, she had a right to talk to me as an outraged intimate.

"I feel alone."

The tone of my voice surprised me. Was I at last, after all this time, going to make her my confessional?

"That is your own stupid affair," she said brusquely, then changing the subject, asked if I was concerned about my sons going off so young to foreign countries.

"I believe Francis learned French at school," I said. "I also believe Thomas has taken the initiative of learning a little Spanish. But even if they haven't, they can get by on their English."

"That is not what I mean," she replied.

"What do you mean, Isabelle?" I paused, and then murmured softly, "What exactly do you mean?"

"The facts of life," she added, turning her head away as if she had said something distasteful.

"Isabelle," I replied, "you were young in the sexual revolution of the sixties, but this is a generation that sends naked photos of themselves to one another on their mobile phones. They lead secret lives on the internet and have God knows how many friends on Face–"

"Facebook!"

She spat out the word contemptuously.

"Well, whatever it is. The names of these places may change, but it's still the same thing. They network socially."

"Nonsense."

Her voice was precise and to the point.

"Both Francis and Thomas have completely open lives. I should know. They are innocents."

"Oh?"

I raised my eyebrows. She looked at me intently.

"You have a dirty mind," she said.

"We can't know for sure what they're up to."

"I am sure," she insisted.

"Then I believe you. But I still say they do know about what you euphemistically call the facts of life. Both the birds and the bees have visited them, I am sure of that. They are at an age of raging hormones and secret pleasures. Think about it."

"They are still children."

"Look at their bodies," I replied dryly.

"I have," she cried defiantly. "They are almost grown-up young men."

"They are young men!"

"Almost," she insisted, "but one thing is for sure. They are still innocents."

"You are naïve, Isabelle," I said rudely. We were in battle now.

"No, I am not naïve. Their mother, before she died, asked me to see they said their prayers."

"What?" I replied.

I got off the bed and came close to her. I must have looked menacing, for she backed away. I was furious. I could have hit her. Her crinkly flesh repelled me, and so now did this sudden odour of sanctity, this brutally sweet odour of faith emanating from Catherine's long-dead corpse.

"She told you what?"

I almost spat the words in her face.

"She told you to make sure they prayed?"

"Yes."

"But Catherine believed in nothing," I said. "Her faith was in name only."

"Maybe you think you knew her religion better than I did, but all the same, she wanted her sons to have a belief. She wanted them to treat their bodies as holy, and to treat women well when they grew up."

"Then why do you question about them going away on their own if they are so morally self-aware?"

"Other people can corrupt," she said obscurely.

We were so close I could smell her breath. It disgusted me so much that I walked away. My gesture was a sign of defeat. She did not want to let go of the fight and shouted after me.

"You don't care if they are corrupted. It is of no concern to you if their innocence is damaged."

"Only God is innocent."

The words seemed to wrench themselves of their own accord from the pit of my stomach. I felt the pain of saying them. As if from a great height I saw both she and I in the room, fighting, and it was absurd. I wanted to kill the old woman, and she it seemed felt somewhere deep within herself a similar desire. We were mutually disgusted by each other, and yet we fought on, and I, from a hidden pit of knowledge I had no knowledge of, proclaimed that God alone was innocent, as if I knew. As if I knew anything.

"I am tired," I muttered. "I want to be left to myself."

"As always," she replied.

The innocence of God had temporarily closed the fight. She began to talk at me in more of a normal tone.

"I believe in their innocence, never mind God's," she said. "But I do not believe they are going to innocent places or that they will meet up with innocent people."

"Then what would you have liked, Isabelle, for them to remain closeted here until marriage? Wasn't it you who suggested they should travel?"

"Yes, but I know they are more or less safe here."

"What do you mean more or less?"

"I am here," she replied, defiant again.

I sensed the resurgence of the battle, and I was too exhausted to endure it or to want it. They were gone and no longer in her control, and perhaps it was best they were gone. At that moment I even wished Francis would escape forever from this closed-in house. Isabelle went to open the door to leave, but I stopped her by asking about Catherine's faith.

"Did she want a priest before she died?" I asked.

Isabelle shook her head.

"I think she realised you would be angry if a priest came here," she said.

"But did she want a priest?"

"I'm not sure she had anything to confess," Isabelle replied quietly. "I am not Catholic, so what do I know about these things? An after-life exists or it doesn't. I don't give it much thought. I expect Catherine, being Catholic, did expect one, but she wasn't afraid. She endured the end with patience, knowing simply that there was nothing to be done about the finality of her suffering."

As she said these last words I heard her begin to sob. She tried to hide her emotion, but the sobbing sounds escaped her nonetheless. The sound revolted me, made me afraid, and unable to control myself I rushed at her and closed her mouth with my hand. I held her tightly as if in an embrace, holding in with force the sound of feeling that I detested. She struggled free and ran from the room. I called after her, appalled suddenly at what I had done, but did not run after her.

I have written this scene out in detail because after that encounter I did not see Isabelle again. She packed her belongings, left no note and placed the keys to the house in the hall. Only recently did I learn that she died a few weeks later at the house of her only sister, from cancer. She had been diagnosed while living in the house with us, but had hidden the fact. Isabelle haunts my dreams along with the other dead, and I know that she will never cease to return to me in them.

A month passed. I began to get tired of living in my dirty clothes and my untidiness. I got tired of the piles of unclean dishes in the kitchen and the dust in the hallways and stairs. I employed a woman to come in once a week to clean; she was called Eva and came from Lithuania. She could hardly speak English, but there was no need for any but the most essential communication between us. I went for long walks, and often returned to the park and the lake. I watched the people around me and did not miss my loss of contact with others. The leaves on the trees turned that deep green that marks the end of summer, that appears to signal their impending browning, their impending fall. I thought about Francis, and as much as I longed to see him again I tried hard not to miss him. As for Thomas I tried to dismiss him altogether from my thoughts, but found he would intrude into them without me willing him to do so. Francis was welcome in my mind as long as I did not feel mental pain, but Thomas was different. He would come to me quite often just as I was about to prepare the bed, and I would see him sitting by the fire reading a book. I dismissed any thought that made me believe I in some way needed him. He came often to my dreams, dressed in various disguises. One night I dreamt I had met a youth I was sexually attracted to, and who was attracted to me. But the youth disgusted me as much as I felt desire for him. With each sexual act I felt a sense of repulsion: at the way he walked, at the way he would talk. I was disgusted by his simpering voice. Then in the dream he took me to a relative's house. The house began to sink into the ground as we approached it, making it almost impossible for us to enter. At last we made our way in through a labyrinthine path that seemed to pass through sewers. Once inside the house I met the sister, a woman over twice his age and old enough to be his mother. She said she had a son and that he would join them soon. Then the scene changed to a party, with a lot of people in the house, and I managed to avoid the youth with whom I was having a sexual relationship. I talked with the sister and a few others, and when the door opened and a young man entered she exclaimed, "Here he is. Here is my son Francis."

Francis came forward and I fell in love immediately. He was radiant in the sewer-smelling place we were in, an angel of light in the dark subterranean world where I was with these new acquaintances. I looked at him and he looked at me. The brightness was almost too much for me. I felt faint with love and yet there was little sexual desire. He came to me and immediately took me by the hand. The touch of his hand only confirmed what I had seen with my eyes. I felt a need to hold on to him literally, to feel him as well as to see him. He was not the Francis who was my son, but another part of myself that I had found, or perhaps even re-found. We sat in silence and he looked at me and held on to my hand. Neither of us cared how many people were looking. I was not concerned that the youth I had had sex with was looking at us. No one else existed except this radiant boy who was a part of me, yet totally other. Then the room darkened, and when the light returned Thomas had taken his place, had taken over his form, and I screamed. I screamed and woke up, my body and my bed drenched with sweat. I showered and let the water wash over me for a long time. I had to wash off Thomas, the intruder in my dream. I needed to wash my flesh, for Thomas's hand had replaced the hand of this young man Francis whom I felt was the love of my life. When I dressed and entered the world of the day, the image of the young man who had disappeared remained. His beauty and his touch pursued me, never for a moment leaving me alone. I longed for sleep so as to find him again, but when I did sleep other dreams came. A week passed, and it was only after six or seven days that the dream memory of him began to fade. But as the memory of the young man Francis faded, Thomas intruded more openly than before. He would follow me down bombed-out streets, follow me through cities destroyed by fire or falling apart with decay. Sometimes I would bump into him as I turned a corner and he would grin at me, and then as quickly as he had come he would slip away, lost in the crowd of those other figures who haunted my dream state. In other dreams he would be the sexual partner in a situation I did not want, yet accepted. He would caress me and beg me to penetrate him, and consistently I would fight against this. I cannot do it, I would cry out, and this too would wake me up. In my new waking madness I would wash several times a day, sometimes scrubbing at my body so hard it would bleed. My mind, both asleep and awake, was in a constant state of turmoil. More and more I wanted to be delivered from myself, even to die if it meant I could stop the waking and sleeping nightmares.

One morning Eva found me sobbing by my bed. She did not ask me any questions, even the simple questions she could have asked. She bathed my brow with cool water and then, having seated me in a chair, made a silent gesture with her hands that she would go and come back. The silent performance amused me, and I began to laugh. She was not offended and even laughed back at me. Half an hour later she returned with a special brew of tea, or to be correct, an infusion. She took a long time in preparing it, and when it was ready she made me drink it. Like a child I accepted her help. A little while later I felt giddy and unwell and went back to bed. The bed rocked as if I was on a rough sea, and this nauseating sensation lasted for what seemed an interminable time. I needed to vomit, to vomit up my life. Visions and people flooded my brain until I felt I could no longer bear it. Certainly death was preferable to this, and I shouted and raved, giving full vent to my fears, but after a while I entered quieter waters, and then I fell into a light but pleasurable sleep. When I at last fully woke, I felt as if I had been purged.

I knew for a while I was safe. I knew whatever it was she had given me in that drink had got rid of a lot of the sickening mess in my mind. As in the dream about falling in love I felt I had had to experience the horrors of the sewer before reaching this oasis of calm. It's true I had no hand to hold or perfect eyes to look into, but I had myself again. I felt whole. Eva had dredged the sewer of my being with her potion, exorcising the filth that lay there, bringing it all to the surface and then out. For a while, I felt I would be able to be in control, both of my waking and my sleeping self. I went to theatres and concerts. I saw exhibitions. I chatted with a few strangers I met in these places and felt once more a part of the human race. I even believed I was at peace with my sons, and in a state of what I thought then was total lucidity told myself I could cope with any eventuality concerning them. I left Eva a little present every week. Sometimes a box of chocolates, sometimes flowers. I even left her a bottle of champagne. This was the only way to thank her for saving me from my demons. After a few weeks of this she would pout and make a face, gesturing that enough was enough and that I did not have to go on like this. She was happy I was happy and pleased to let it end there. Eventually, I got the point and stopped leaving her things. She cleaned and went, as silently as she had before.

The crash came. Not from inside but from outside. Just as I was in balance with myself, I toppled. As I have mentioned I have an aversion to the new technologies. I did not have a mobile phone and nor did I possess a computer. My sons had both, but they had taken them with them. There was only the old and very old-fashioned looking single phone in the living room. One evening in mid-September it rang. No one rang me, so I was shocked to hear it sound. I picked it up and felt an intuitive fear. This is going to be bad.

I heard Thomas's voice.

"Father, it's Thomas. I'm in Paris. I came up from Barcelona to meet with Francis, but he has disappeared from his hotel. I even had to pay his hotel bill."

He spoke rapidly and far too quickly, as if he was being hounded by someone, overheard.

"I don't like Paris," he added before I had a chance to speak. "The city makes me afraid."

"Where are you staying?"

He named the hotel.

"How long has Francis been missing?"

"Two weeks."

"Why didn't you contact me before?"

"I did. There was always no reply. Where the hell were you?"

I realised I had been out a lot recently, high on my recovery and regaining what I called my sanity. Somehow I could find no words to tell him that. The thought of this impossibility made me laugh.

"Why are you laughing? Are you laughing at me?"

"No, at me," I replied.

"Are you alright?"

"No," I said simply, suddenly finding the words to tell him. "I was quite mad, or so I thought, and then I recovered. A woman gave me a herbal drink and restored my sanity."

"Father, you are joking."

"Yes, Thomas, I am joking," I said. "Let's just say I was out most of the time."

"Isn't Isabelle there?"

"She left. Family problems. I want to leave it at that."

"You mean she has gone for good?"

"I think so." Then I added, "Yes, Thomas, she has gone for good. I don't think she liked me very much and decided with you two gone –"

"But not for good…" he interrupted.

"Well, let's put it like this, she left because she was only fond of you two, and now you are on the road to manhood she felt she was no longer needed."

"Father, you are talking nonsense. What do you mean, you are not alright?"

"Thomas, this is about Francis, not me. I am coming to Paris."

"You?"

He sounded startled.

"I can travel, Thomas," I replied. "I too am capable of travelling."

There was a moment of silence before he answered.

"I'm glad. I'm glad you're coming to Paris."

"Can you give me the address of your hotel?"

It was one of a chain of hotels, this one situated just ten minutes from the Gare du Nord. I also took his room number and the telephone number of the hotel. Before we parted on the phone he lightly reprimanded me for not having a mobile phone. He added I was not old and I should get used to the new century. I did not make any reply.

"Will you use a mobile phone if I buy it for you?" he asked.

"We will see," I said.

"When do you think you will come?"

"Tomorrow, if I can get down to London and find a seat for Paris. If not, within the next couple of days. I will leave a message at the hotel and confirm arrival."

We said our goodbyes and I put down the phone.

Francis. Disappeared.

The horror has begun, I thought. This time the nightmares will come from without and not from within. It was like a death to me, this thought of going to Paris. I felt like a dog having to return to the grave of some master it has hated. To scratch with wounded paws at the grave of this dead master who was somehow still alive, still calling from the coffin below. I hated Paris, and yet in my early twenties I had been there and seen death there. I had seen the death of feeling in a succession of automatic passions: mechanical passions with men who introduced me to a pain that somehow led on to the further pain of my marriage. As I sat and thought about Francis having disappeared there, I felt the biting word of death, my own death towards passion and the expression of love. I had gone there when I was young to explore and to see. Yes, that was it. That was it. There was a darkness in my dream of sending my son to France. In my unconscious self I was sending Francis to explore his passions, to find his pain, and now I had heard that he had disappeared, that Paris had swallowed him up, had made him disappear. And I, when I had dreamt of him going, of his taking Hemingway, I had sent him on a death tour. I shuddered and closed up these subterranean thoughts. And I remembered my own self in my twenties, older than him but just as innocent, just as open to whatever would come. I tried so hard after I left Paris to leave it behind me, to have it as a grave I would not have to return to. But my son, my son who I desired and loved was lost there, lost in that living graveyard, and I had to go to try and find him. I only hoped Paris had not been a master to him, overpowering him as it had overpowered me. I hoped he had been able to hurt, was still able wherever he was, either in that terrible city or elsewhere, to hurt and not be hurt. Not to be mastered as I had been mastered, not to be made to grovel like a dog as I had been made to grovel. To be at the call of people who only knew words of abuse, never of tenderness: people who despised the youths they desired. I had known so many of them in their various false disguises of lovers. People who wanted the sensual gratification of sex with young men, but none of the tenderness. The tenderness was never there, and I only hoped Francis had not experienced that emptiness of un-tender love.

One man especially I remembered. His name was Christophe. He was from the south of France and dark, almost black with his dark skin tone and his curly black hair. He had attracted me the most and he had pretended to love me, all the time seeing his women and giving them the tenderness he denied me. He gave me an imitation of gentleness, an imitation of gentle reaching out, but when it came to the actual contact of his body I only felt a hard core of hating. He took from me, took every position of physical lovemaking from me and then threw it back at me like a bone for me to eat. He had taunted me with his women. He was not queer: I was the queer. The queer English boy who was willing to nuzzle against his skin and look at him with adoring eyes. I was his puppy to be touched and made much of, and then to be kicked and shouted at. In the end, after he had used me up and abused me enough, he got married. The marriage was sudden. The woman was pregnant and he wanted a son. A real son, not a young man who was a child at heart. He had hated the child in me and had hurt and hurt, until all innocence and hope had bled out of me. And still I stayed on in the city. Still I went with other men, similar to him, most of them sneering at their own homosexuality and at mine. They only had hatred for the desire that felt, and I was easy to hate and easy to hurt. It took a long time for me to break away, to come back to England and close the memories off. To bury them deep in the grave that was within myself. I had gone as an innocent to Paris and had returned to England soiled and despising my desire. The worst of it is I lie to myself about this episode, this defining episode of my youthful life. I pretend it never existed, that the grave of the place does not exist. I pretend so much I was not murdered in my heart. How is it then that I am capable of sending my own son off to France?

These thoughts raced through my mind as I hurried about my business of buying a Eurostar ticket and of leaving a note for Eva to explain I would be gone for an unspecified period of time. I would try not to think again of my Paris, of the Paris I had lived, but to see it in the present tense, to see it as only a foreign territory that had reached out for my lost son.

Part Two
Paris

Lost. How could he be lost?

I was on the train, deep in the tunnel that separates England from France. I gazed out of the window into darkness and I felt afraid. My hands shook as I drank some coffee. I wanted to be there, in Paris, quickly and then be gone. I wanted to see Francis's face and see his hair blow again in the wind. I wanted him to be alright and not to be hurt. Above all I wanted him not to be hurt. Then I was out of the tunnel, oblivious to the beauty of the Normandy countryside. I closed my eyes to it and only opened them as the train arrived at the Gare du Nord.

The first thing I saw on the station were warnings about the dangers of flu. Paris was in the middle of an epidemic and care was needed; preventions had to be taken. I looked in panic at the written words and wondered if Francis had fallen suddenly ill, had been taken urgently to hospital. It was in this state of panic that I met Thomas at the hotel. He was waiting in the foyer.

"Was the journey alright?" he asked.

I brushed away the question with an irritated gesture of my hand.

"Have you searched the hospitals?" I asked. I didn't even notice my other son. I did not even call him by his name. There was nothing kind in my voice.

"Yes, Father, I have," he said. "He is not in any of them."

"It's this flu –"

"I know," he added, "but he is not in any of the hospitals. The government is exaggerating the epidemic anyway. It is not as bad as they say."

"I don't care about that. I just want to be sure he is not in some hospital. Maybe there is some obscure hospital you do not know about."

"Father, you are crazy. There is no such thing as an obscure hospital that Francis might be in."

"A clinic then."

"He would not have been taken to a clinic."

"How do you know?"

"I know."

His voice was getting louder, more impatient with me.

"There are a lot of clinics in Paris," I insisted. "A lot of private ones that are not that well known. Obscure places –"

"That word again! Obscure!" He laughed the word back at me. "Obscurity is for dreams and darkness. You are here with me in the light of Paris, Father, and there are no obscure hospitals or clinics he has been taken to. Trust me."

I sat down in one of the foyer chairs. I was exhausted. I had not slept the previous night. I wanted to avoid the possibility of nightmares. Thomas looked down at me, and there was a weariness in him too as he said, "We would have been contacted if he had been admitted to a hospital."

"You would think so," I said.

"But then again," he added, "I wanted to be sure. There can be confusions."

I looked up at Thomas.

"Confusions? What are you talking about?"

"Nothing. I have reserved you a room on the same floor as mine. It's not a very good hotel, but there are much worse in Paris."

"Someone here might know something," I said slowly. "Have you questioned anybody?"

Thomas sat down next to me. He passed his hand over his face, as if he was wiping away a cobweb. His fingers looked long and thin. He had lost weight and it showed in his face.

"I have talked to several people. There was one man he was apparently friendly with, but he is away now. He will be back in a few days' time. As for Francis's things, they have been locked away. I also informed the police of his disappearance, but they say he may have just gone off to stay somewhere else for a while."

"Did he take anything with him?"

"No."

Thomas paused. It was obvious he was getting tired of my questioning.

"Nothing at all to indicate he may have gone to stay somewhere else?"

"I told you, no."

His voice was sharp.

"Sorry, Thomas," I replied. "I haven't even asked you how you are taking all this."

"That's alright, Father. I didn't expect you to."

He got up then, walked away from me and talked to a woman behind the desk. She handed him the pass for the room. He came back and handed it to me.

"You look as if you need to rest," he said. "We can meet at seven for dinner. The food is simple here, but serviceable. I presume you don't want to go out into Paris tonight. I know I don't."

He sighed then, huddling into himself. He was dressed all in black. A black suit, sweater, accentuating his dark good looks. His face was white though, and as I said, thinner than I had seen it before.

"Are you ill?" I asked. "You look pale. Black is good on you, but maybe not when you look so white."

"I was sick for a while in Barcelona," he said. "A sort of flu. It kept me in bed for a while. As much as I dislike Paris I wanted a change and that's when I arranged to come up and see Francis. That was over three weeks ago when I was getting better." He paused. "I sent Francis a message a couple of times, but I didn't pay any attention to getting no answer. But let's not talk about it anymore for now."

He smiled at me, a charming smile that broke up his morose look. He came alive in his smile, and his voice was almost flirtatious, as if seeking a compliment when he said, "When the sun was out and hot in Barcelona, I was ill, and when I got better it rained and rained. That's why I am so pale and uninteresting. I would have liked to have looked better for you."

I turned away, embarrassed almost at this need for closeness. I wanted to tell him his good looks had not changed, and that he looked fine despite the paleness. But the words would not come. They felt ridiculously indecent.

I went to my room. It was neutral. Above my bed was the sort of inoffensive rubbish hotels always put on walls. A landscape with snow, and a church in the distance. A desk coming out of the wall to write on, and a chair. A sickly muddy brown everywhere. Only the white of the painted snow alleviated the brown splodge of the hotel landscape, but the room would do. I thought of Francis then and how his room must have been the same. Only the picture would probably have been different, but then again it was possible even that was the same as mine. I laughed as I imagined every room in this hotel to have the same painting – the wonders of the art of mechanical reproduction.

I rested, but I could not sleep. I faced a television on the wall opposite the bed, but I had no desire to turn it on. Then at half-six I washed and got ready for dinner. I had brought a small suitcase with no change of clothes, except for underwear and socks. I was dressed in a light grey suit, and on top of that, a white mackintosh. Even my tie was grey. I thought with grim irony that both Thomas and myself had somehow dressed appropriately for a funeral.

"I don't feel up to this trip," Thomas said at dinner.

I looked at his face. I saw a very young man trying hard to be an older man, part succeeding and part failing. He was seventeen and too young to cope with what was happening. And his illness in Spain? What had that meant? As a father I should have cared more, shown more. I felt barren inside. Hollow. Empty of any need to try and yet at the same time I knew I was wrong in feeling this.

"I should have done what you have done," I said feebly. "I should have shown more – how shall I put it – ?"

I fumbled with the words.

"– understanding about how Francis's disappearance is affecting you. After all, so far you have spent your whole life with him, however different in character you may or may not be."

"Yes, we are different," he murmured quietly, "but deep down there is a sameness in the difference that is hard to explain."

"Not at all. You are brothers. All brothers must feel like that." Then I added, "I never had brothers or sisters. Well, you know that. No tedious Christmas cards or boring letters from aunts or uncles on my side of the family."

"None on my mother's side either," he said quickly, looking at me.

As if ashamed, I could not face his look and turned my head away. We spent the rest of the meal picking at our food, not really eating. It was a mixture of meat and salad and looked pathetically cold on the plate.

"Shall we have coffee?" I asked eventually.

"Father," he cried out suddenly. "He has gone. He has gone for good. I know it. I can't pretend any longer about this. He wanted to get away from both of us."

Something shrank inside of me at these words. They made me feel sick. There was a truth in them that jabbed at me, hurting me, making me withdraw.

"You don't know that. You have no evidence for that," I replied coldly.

"When I was sick, and asked him if I could come to see him, he asked me why I should want to. He asked if I wasn't happy that at last we were all separated from each other."

"He meant for a time, not for always."

"No, there was something in his voice."

The waiter came then and hovered over us. I ordered

coffee and he moved slowly away, glancing once behind his back at us. He was not much older than Thomas, and in a moment I could tell he was interested in Thomas. The glance back was at him, not at me. I wondered if he was wondering if we were lovers. Older man and younger man. Easy to think.

"Francis did not want me to come but he did not dare say it."

"That would not make him want to disappear and leave all his things behind, even if it were true, which I doubt." I paused, and then said, "but I can understand he was glad to be away from me. There was no love there on his side."

"Was there on yours?"

An old man took the place of the teenage boy. An old, knowing look was in his expression. I did not believe this younger son of mine was as inexperienced as he professed to be.

"I love him."

The words were said simply. I wished the waiter would return quickly with the coffee. I needed to eat or drink something. I did not want to be trapped at the table with nothing to do with my hands. I needed to cover the love I was feeling. And yet at the same time an inner voice, a harsh inner voice, was jeering at me. *You call it love*, the voice said, *but it is naked desire. It is a desire to see him naked and open to your lust for him. Call it love if you will.*

"I thought you did," Thomas said slowly.

He was flushed in the face by the clear tone of my declaration. I knew he was not sure what to do with it, how to reply.

"Did you ever tell him you loved him?" he asked after a long silence. The waiter was just putting the coffee on the table as he spoke and looked at Thomas as he said these words. He smiled, and I saw he had heard everything clearly. He glanced back again at the table after he had left us, and this time met my eye. Flustered, he accelerated his step towards the kitchen. I turned back to Thomas, but before I could reply he said, "No, don't tell me. I don't want to know."

"Why?"

He shook his head in silence and drank his coffee very quickly.

"Thomas, I asked why?"

"I can't –" he began, and then stopped.

I drank my much-needed coffee slowly to give him time. Suddenly I was interested in him and really did want to know why. I peeked at him over the rim of my coffee cup as I drank the last drop. There were beads of perspiration on his forehead. He was staring down at the table, and at the remains of what we had consumed.

"Look at me please, Thomas."

The order was said softly, but firmly. It was a mixture of paternal command and the demand of a lover. After a short while he brushed at the sweat on his brow and mumbled what he had to say as low as possible.

"I wanted you to say it to me. So much. For so long."

He clutched at the sides of the table with his hands as if he wanted to lift it off the ground. I had an image of him lifting the flimsy dinner table and then flinging it in frustration and anger across the room. I sensed there was a lot of potential violence in those young hands. Clutching hard, he repeated what he had just said, but now loudly.

"I wanted you to say it to me. So much. For so long."

"I heard you, Thomas," I replied as gently as I could.

His voice shook as he said, "It's because I never really knew you, I suppose. I had lots of fantasies about you. When I was a kid. When I was younger."

And now? I said the words to myself, but said nothing to him, letting him get it all out if he wanted to. I knew he was under strain over Francis and that he was showing that strain. Maybe the disappearance of his brother had suddenly given him an inward permission to make this confession.

"It's strange," he continued, "because I know you're not much good."

"Thank you," I said, showing a mocking but all the same sincere sarcasm.

"Don't get me wrong," he added.

"I don't think I'm much good either," I threw at him with a smile.

"It's about mother, I suppose, and about Isabelle. Isabelle really did dislike you. I can say that now I know she has left. She would often refer to your mysterious cruelties, but she would never elaborate. She would insinuate, but never be clear. She let us imagine awful things. Francis was perhaps affected the most by this."

"Thank you for telling me all this," I said, and my tone of voice now sounded strangely polite. I looked at my son. He had wanted my love and I had ignored him. This I recognised only too well and also how much they must have been talked at by Isabelle. And yet the truth, beneath all the complexities and all the sexual confusions, I was not a good man. Had I once been good, a long time ago when I was but a few years older than him and learning from men? Or had these men sensed it was just a veneer to be stamped out by cruelties and in so doing taught me how to be more cruel even than them? In my mind I saw Catherine lying on a bed writhing beneath my body, hating it, knowing as she did know that I was only using her and that my violent sex was but a manifestation of that. It is easy to blame others for being responsible for our refinements of cruelty.

"Now I don't want to say another thing," Thomas said. "I am strung out and anxious, and you really should not listen to me at all."

"I will pay the bill," I said quietly, and went immediately to do it. Once paid I waited at the front of the restaurant. Thomas came up to me after a short while.

"I'll say goodnight, Father," he said.

I caught his arm as he moved away from me, and as he turned I saw a look on his face I had never seen before. It was a look bright with expectancy, bright with a need for me to say what he needed to hear. I saw in that look, that having now exposed his past feeling of love, the love was still there. It shone brightly now, in an open look of hope.

"I want to know what our plans are for tomorrow," I said. "I don't want to detain you any further."

His faced dimmed. The brightness died. I had killed it with my words: such simple words, and yet in their banality as cutting as any knife.

"You make the plans," he replied.

He smiled weakly and walked away.

The following morning there was a note waiting for me at the desk. Thomas had simply written that he would be out all day and would meet me in the evening at the same time for dinner. Rightly or wrongly I interpreted this note as a need to avoid seeing me. I screwed up the note and put it in my pocket. I felt alone, and above all alone with Paris. Slowly I made my way to the entrance, smelled the familiar Paris smells and walked out into the street.

I caught the metro to Etienne Marcel. I was crushed in a carriage with a group of Japanese people, most of them with white masks covering the lower part of their faces. A young Japanese boy bumped accidentally against my legs and looked up anxiously. His eyes had fear in them. His look seemed to say to me: Why aren't you wearing a mask? Are you sick already? Don't you care? I smiled down at him and he turned away, pushing through the legs of his fellow travellers until he found the woman he was with. I struggled out of the carriage at Etienne Marcel and made my way to the surface. It was not far for me to walk to Beaubourg, to the place where I had spent so many days in my youth. The place in front of the Centre Pompidou looked the same, yet changed. The sense of exhilaration, of fun in the streets, had gone. The freshness had gone out of it all. I walked around until I found the building where the Café Costes had been. It had been there that I had encountered people, there and in the sex cinemas. I wondered if they still existed. The sun was strong and I felt dismally chilled: chilled at the memory of those arenas of physical despair. From the Place des Innocents where the Café Costes had been I made my way to Forum des Halles and descended into the hell of the shops below. I wandered around the FNAC and picked out a DVD I thought I wanted, changed my mind and put it back again. It was a copy of *l'Homme blessé*, a film I had seen several times and had liked, but I needed air and soon I regained the surface and went into the church of Saint Eustace. The gothic splendour of it had inspired me once, but now I found the columns and the perspectives just a jungle of old stone I wanted to get out of. I laughed as I wondered where God could possibly be lurking, there in that jungle.

I felt aimless and walked aimlessly. I crossed over to the left bank, and it was there that I saw him in the distance. I saw the back of his head first and his fair hair. He moved his head slightly, and there before he turned into the rue Saint-Sulpice I definitely saw Francis. Like Jacob in the painting by Delacroix in the church of Saint-Sulpice I hurried to struggle with my angel. I ran so as not to miss him, so as not to give him any more time to disappear from me again. I reached the turning into the rue Saint-Sulpice, and as I did so I saw him go through the door of a dark house on same side of the street as the church. I hurried forward and reached the door, now closed. I pushed at the door and it opened. A corridor of darkness stretched in front of me leading to winding stairs that led from floor to floor. I heard steps, and knowing they would soon stop and enter one of the apartments I ran as fast as I could up the twisting, wooden stairs. On the third landing, darkened because it had no window to lighten it, an equally dark figure was standing at a door. Frantic with anticipation, I threw myself at the figure, clutching the body with my hands, holding it to me. The figure shouted and pushed, and then I found myself on the ground. I looked up and a young man who in no way resembled Francis stared down at me. How could I have been mistaken? I had seen him. I was sure I had seen him in the distance. I knew the son I loved and could not have made a mistake. This other, dark young man looked down at me.

"Who are you?" he shouted. Then he added quickly, "Get up, you look ridiculous."

I stood. I felt giddy and reached for the wall to steady myself.

"I was mistaken," I said, my throat tight and barely able to speak.

"Were you following me?"

"Yes."

The wooden floor began to tilt up towards me. I was going to faint. I cried out. I heard a voice say, "Are you ill?" and then I was in a black void. I plunged into the inward night of myself, and as I fell inwards I saw Francis smile at me. A moment later the falling vision was gone. I was still and cold and trapped, as aware as if I had been buried alive in a coffin. I was conscious in my unconsciousness and felt that final horror one must feel when one knows there is a finality, and no escape. I tried to cry out, but the sound was sucked back into my conscious emptiness, into the hollow nothingness I had become. This is for all eternity. This is the constant death that has no end.

"Do you want water?"

I heard words. I saw light. I struggled to replace my inward consciousness for the consciousness of the world. My eyes were open, but as yet I saw nothing but a harsh whiteness, a blinding white.

"Don't be afraid."

I was staring up at a white overhead light. A figure stepped between me and the light, casting a shadow of darkness over my uncertain sight. I thought, I don't want to go inwards again. I don't want to be imprisoned again. A hand touched my forehead, then the shadow moved away, and finally I saw a young, dark face looking down at me. I realised I was lying full out on a sofa.

"You fainted, and I brought you into my apartment."

"Thank you." I managed to mumble the words, and then found myself murmuring, "You are not Francis. I thought you were him."

"Be quiet. You have been out for a long time. First drink this."

He raised my head with one hand, and then gently made me drink from a glass of water with the other.

"My name is Benoît," he said.

I stared at his face as I drank. I drank all of the water. He asked if I wanted some more and I shook my head. Even lying down I felt dizzy, but at the same time I felt better. I knew that soon I would be alright, that the attack would be over.

"It was my expectancy," I said slowly. "I expected you to be him, and when I saw –"

"No more now," he interrupted, "just lie still and be quiet."

"But I'm beginning to feel better," I said. "It's just I made a mistake. I saw blond hair, when you have dark hair, and I followed."

"Does he live here?"

"It seems not," I said quietly.

"So you were looking for someone, and you thought I was him."

It sounded so simple the way he said the words, but the terrible reality remained. I thought I had found Francis, and now he was as lost to me as when I first came to Paris. I shifted on the sofa and put myself into a sitting position. I faced a white wall and a brightly coloured painting. With absurd clarity I saw it had no subject. It was a mass of black and red lines tangled together. In my troubled state it looked like an abstract scene of violence. The reduction of violence itself to its basic red and black: like a car crash or a fight, like a stabbing in the dark when blood covers everything. At the heart of its lack of subject it had the violence of all suffering and in my pained mind all of brutal death itself.

"It is true," I said.

"What?"

He sat down on a chair in front of the sofa and stared at me.

"The painting."

I pointed to the wall facing me. He had his back to it.

"You like it?" he said. "I bought it in Portugal. My parents live in Lisbon."

"I have never been to Lisbon."

I did not want to get into conversation. Now the mistake had been explained, and the force of my reaction to it had passed, I felt embarrassed. I shook my head from side to side and closed my eyes. I wanted permission to go. When I opened my eyes I saw the young man was looking intently into them. He was darkly handsome, and chilled and ill though I was, I found him desirable.

"I have never been followed before," he said. His voice was almost a whisper. Instinctively, I felt there was a possibility for sex in this situation, and that I needed it.

"It was a mistake," I repeated.

I stared back into his eyes, conscious that my look was saying something totally different.

"Was it such a mistake?"

He reached out with his hand and touched my arm lightly. Instinct again told me that perhaps he had had little experience, that I had been a shock on the landing, but now in his apartment not such a disagreeable surprise. He let his hand remain lightly on my arm. This was now a clear, unspoken invitation.

"We could lie down in my bedroom," he said.

His voice shook, betraying a certain fear.

"Perhaps I need a little more rest," I replied.

He took his hand away and stood. I looked at him now with open desire. I looked at his denim jeans, at the firmness of his young legs.

"How old are you?" I asked.

"Eighteen," he replied.

"I am more than old enough to be your father."

He smiled, and when he next spoke he seemed sincere.

"I like men of your age, and you are an attractive man."

"I passed out on your landing. That cannot have been attractive."

"It showed vulnerability," he replied. "Perhaps it is odd to say, but that made you even more desirable."

For one brief moment I had to be honest with him. I had to tell him why I had run after him.

"I have a son of your age," I said. "He has disappeared in Paris. I am here in Paris with his brother, my other son, to look for him. There was a trick of the light, and I really thought you were him."

"Do we have the same sort of body, your son and I?" he enquired, looking down at himself, looking at the swelling in his jeans that was now visibly showing his desire.

His look down made me look down. In my mind I imagined that yes, it was Francis I had found. It was Francis, standing there, displaying himself.

"You have a different complexion and hair. He is not dark."

"Yet you thought I was him?"

There was a tender mockery in the question. He began to take off his shirt as his spoke, undoing each button slowly as he spoke.

"For a second I was sure you were him," I said.

"How much you must desire him," he whispered. Then he added, "Do you desire him?"

"I can't say that."

"Tell me the truth. It excites me. I want to be your fantasy for the little time we will have together. In a few hours' time I have to go out with a girl my parents want me to marry."

He took off his shirt and let it fall to the floor. His body was as trim and as firm as Francis's. He had a small amount of dark hair around his nipples, and a long exciting line of hair that led to his groin.

"We can do it here if you like," he said, and then before I could reply he had taken off his jeans. He was naked beneath them, and his sex swelled out. I took it in my hand.

"Is your son like me – there?" he asked.

"I imagine him to be equally beautiful," I said, and then hungrily took the flesh in my mouth. Took it to the point of suffocation, wanting to die in desire for the memory of my son who was lost to me.

All through the acts of fellation and anal penetration I had Francis firmly, excitingly in my mind. At last I was possessing him, opening him up. I even called out his name at the moment of climax, and as I did so the dark boy beneath me laughed with pleasure. He then clutched my body tightly with one arm, making himself come with his free hand as he did so. He cried out "Father" in my arms.

The word uttered, revealed, made me shrink from him. I felt a sudden sense of horror and shame. I got up and hurriedly put on my clothes.

"Father, why are you running away so quickly? It was good and my girl can wait. Can't we do it again? Don't you want to come inside your son again?"

It was like an hallucination. I imagined Francis himself jeering at me, laughing at me. I felt sick and asked where the bathroom was. Once inside it I vomited into the sink, not being quick enough to get to the toilet. Then I rinsed my mouth out and gurgled with some mouthwash I had found by the bath. After I had finished I sensed him behind me, and with a sideways look I saw him step into the bath and turn on the shower that was hanging over it. Hot water from the shower splashed over me. I turned to face him and he smiled at me through the falling rush of water.

"We should do it here," he cried, and began to playfully splash at my face and clothes with the water.

I dodged away and out into the living room. In a few minutes I was completely ready to leave and left the apartment before he had time to come out of the shower. I ran down the wooden steps with the same urgency as I had run up them.

I made my way back to the hotel. The nausea I had felt in the Saint-Sulpice apartment was returning. Hurriedly, I wrote a message for Thomas, explaining I would not be able to meet him for dinner; I was ill and needed to get some sleep as soon as possible. My writing was a scrawl, and I felt indeed that I had a fever. I wrote that I hoped I would be well enough to join him for breakfast in the morning. Somehow I made it to my hotel room. I threw myself onto the bed with my clothes still on. I had a sudden horror of my own nakedness, and anyway I was cold, so cold, despite the sensation of fever and the suppressed desire to vomit. I fell asleep almost immediately.

My sleep was tormented by visions. I was in Paris, yet it was another city. I was in all the cities of the world, yet enclosed in a room that contained all these cities. In that vast but suffocating space I realised I was not alone. I had another with me. I knew who it was instantly, but refused to name him. I wanted to escape, but one part of the room only led me back to the same place. I ran from the presence and stood still at the same time. I ran from Paris, to London, to Vienna. I crossed great inner plains and saw that they were travelling, but I was still contained, entombed with the one man I most wanted to get away from. My father. The other was my father. Unable to escape in space I tried to escape in time. I shouted at him. I screamed at him.

"Let me return to the time when I was never yours," I cried. "Let me go back so far that I will never, ever meet you in time." But in my futile attempt to avoid time and place I only exhausted my soul; exhausted it into acknowledgement. I was with him and there was no way out. In a last act of refusal I accused him of not being my father.

"I have two sons," I shouted, "but I have no father."

He was clothed in grey clothes, and his face was grey. His hair was also grey, and I could not see his features clearly. I only saw piercing grey eyes staring at me, and two thin lips parting as they spoke my name. I threw myself upon him, but he was elusive and I had the impression I was fighting aged rags, winding clothes that had somehow escaped from a grave. At one point I held him close, held him tight so as to press all breath of ancient life out of him. I wanted to kill him in that room, which was the room of all the cities of the world, but still he would neither die nor leave me. He stuck to me like grey glue, like the smell of sperm on rotting garments.

"You are my son, Francis," he said as he clung to me in the fight. But as we battled on that terrible dark plain of the soul I felt with sharp despair how desperate he was for my love. How passionate he was for my embrace. He was now no longer elusive. He wanted me, wanted me totally. I tried to pierce his body with my cries, tried to throw him off with my revulsion. I hated him and was full of my own desire to murder him.

"Is there no end?"

I screamed the words and tore at his grey face with my fingers, tearing at the papery skin with my nails. I felt the blood flow, and in that instant I was awake in my bed in the hotel room, drinking water from a bottle that was beside my bed. I glanced briefly at the grey light of the window before tumbling back into the world of my dream. I was once more in the room I had briefly left by awakening. He was there, and I was his prisoner, struggling in his arms. He told me he would be eternally there, and that even if I escaped the room he would fight me in the open. He told me the whole outer world would be a place of devastation for our battle, and that he would fight. I gave in then. I fell away from him, falling back onto the mosaic that was all the tortured streets of the cities of the world. I called for a doctor to give me something, anything to prevent me from going insane. I was lying flat on my back and he, my father, towered over me.

"There will be no doctors," he shouted down at me, "but there will be the police. If you do not love me, I will denounce you."

"Then I will be free of you," I cried back. "Call the police, let them come."

He moved away from me, and there in this kaleidoscope of all the hotels in existence he rang a number. He dialled a number on a giant grey phone and told whoever it was at the other end that I was a monster. He told whoever the unknown listener was that he had given birth to a monster and that he was locked in. With these words he showed that our roles were reversed. Suddenly he was the prisoner, and I was the one who had captured. He yelled that I must let him go, that we were poison to each other, but still even in this reversal he would not open the door; still he would not release me. I watched the grey phone move away from him, grow legs and run away. The phone in the room could escape, but not me. Then as if it had never been, it ceased to be. The agony of being imprisoned with him was suddenly over, and I awoke again. I saw the grey had turned to white at the window, and that it was dawn. Then an invisible hand covered my face and I was plunged under. I dreamt I was in my coffin and that the heavy duvet, far too heavy for late summer, was in fact my burial cloth.

This is the way to the crematorium.

The words entered my head, my pounding head that had a pain so intense it was beyond all headaches, beyond all pains I had felt there. I struggled to get free from the bed, from my prison bed, and from the eventual flames that were waiting for me.

"Father, we will burn together," I cried, and at that moment regained full consciousness.

I staggered out of bed and for a long time I stood under a cold shower, begging for the mercy of being cold once again. Shivering at last, I turned off the tap and dried my body. With shaking hands I put on my clothes and left the hotel room.

I wandered down the corridor that led to Thomas's room. I needed to wake him, to talk to him. I needed the reality of him. Remnants of my nightmare remained in my mind, and like floaters in an ageing eye, darkened my vision. I knew the grey, broken cells of my dead father's body would always be there, drifting shadows of a battle-weary desire.

I was about to raise my hand to knock on Thomas's door when I heard sounds coming from within his room. It was the sound of a voice, but I heard it as if it was metallic. A metallic robot voice, repeating over and over, "Yes, yes, yes."

It seemed to come from a machine within Thomas's room, and I wondered why he was not turning the machine off, or answering the voice with his own. I pounded on the door, gripped by a fear that he was in danger, that he was in the presence of an unknown force and could not be delivered from it.

"Thomas," I shouted. "Open the door."

But there was no answer, nothing but the metallic voice saying yes, yes, yes, as if it were repeating in its high-pitched machine tone an affirmation of orgasm, of ecstasy. The sound appalled me, and I was conscious of people hurrying by me along the corridor. I was behaving insanely, and rightly they must have thought I was mad.

"Please," I said, and then lowered my fists.

I backed away from the door, backed away from my son's door, and turning, ran to the lift to take me to the ground floor.

When I reached the breakfast room I found him there. He was alone in the room with a tray of used plates and cups in front of him.

"You are late," he said. "They are ready to clear away."

I looked at him in surprise. I had woken early. Dawn had just broken, and I had not been long in leaving the room. It could be no later than half-seven: the time when the breakfast room opened, not closed.

"What time is it?" I asked.

"Nearly half-ten."

I looked at the clock on the wall. Yes, it was nearly half-past ten. A black woman entered the room and started taking away the food. Thomas called to her and asked her to delay for a few more minutes, explaining that I was his father and had overslept.

"It can't be true, Thomas."

I sat on a chair facing him. He looked at me and shook his head slowly.

"Father, you overslept," he said.

He then reminded me that I had been unwell; that I had remained in my room all of the day before and even the cleaning women had not been allowed to go in to disturb me.

"I was not in my room yesterday," I said. "I was out in Paris. I even thought I –"

I was about to tell him what had happened on the rue Saint-Sulpice, but stopped. I had gone with that boy. The memory and the realisation of it was like a shock to my body. My mind felt distorted.

"I wrote a note for you when I got back," I said, "explaining I would not see you for dinner but see you here for breakfast. I came back to the hotel –"

Thomas interrupted me by laying his hand on mine across the table. It was an intimate gesture that made me draw my hand away. I felt ashamed, but was too confused and irritated by him to want to continue talking. Let him believe what he wants, I thought. I know I am in Paris and that I went with that boy.

"You are obviously still tired despite the long rest in your room."

I looked at him sullenly and said nothing. He got up from the table and prepared my breakfast. I watched with nausea as he put down a cup filled with tea. The nausea continued as he placed a plate full of croissants beside it.

"I can't eat or drink anything," I said. The words were mumbled.

"But after all this time you must be hungry."

"I came down to find you, that's all."

"Well, I have been here for a good hour. I nearly came to your room."

"Funny, I came to yours."

"When?"

"Just before coming down here. I heard a voice from inside. A strange metallic voice."

He laughed at this and put sugar in my tea. I watched as he stirred the cup.

"It must have been part of a dream you couldn't leave behind in your room," he said.

I brushed at my face with my hand, as if to brush the feeling of madness away that was threatening me. What did Thomas mean by saying I had been shut up in my hotel room all of the previous day? And I had heard that relentless crying out of yes, yes, yes from his room. People had seen me pounding on his door. I had made a loud disturbance.

"I was seen pounding on your door," I said. I was now beginning to feel stupid.

"Really," he replied. "Now please eat or drink something. I want you well today. The nightmare is reaching its end."

I looked at him, startled by the words.

"Nightmare? What do you know of it?"

He leant back in his chair and looked at me steadily.

"I have heard from him," he said simply. "Francis rang me yesterday, but I didn't want to disturb you. I thought that yesterday you were perhaps not quite up to knowing what is, in some ways, good news."

"Some ways?"

I looked at him questioningly. There was a darkness in this I did not want to go into. A returning darkness. Despite my terrible night I wanted the light of day. To breathe air. Above all I needed to shake off the coffin clothes. Those of my dead father and potentially of myself.

"There is something dark in this," I murmured.

"Drink your tea at least," he said. "For me."

"Damn you," I replied angrily. "I'm not a child. Don't talk to me like a child. I don't want this breakfast. I want to breathe."

I got up unsteadily from the table and stood there, looking down at Thomas. His face upturned towards me struck me as being heart-breakingly beautiful. Why did I not love this youth? The question jabbed at my brain. I saw his fine dark looks and his sensitivity (yes, it was there) towards me. Call it love if you will, but he felt something towards me his brother had never felt. These thoughts rushed through my mind, and suddenly I said to him, "I am sorry for brushing away your hand."

"When?"

"Just now. When you reached across the table. It's my mind. I don't want to explain. My mind is not as it should be."

I paused. God, I thought, why are there no better words?

"I also know you have done your best. Are you doing your best?"

"I understand, I think," he said. "I mean, it's difficult. What do I know really? It is all strange. All of it. Your relationship to both of us. To Francis and me. It's not easy to say the right thing."

"There is no right thing."

I said these words with emphasis. I knew there would be things he would tell me that would upset, hurt. The darkness covering Francis was implicit in the few words he had said about hearing from him.

"Do you want to go out?" he asked.

"Just to the reception area for the moment. It's brighter than this room. I hate the sight of all this food. I really am disgusted by the sight of it."

"I shouldn't have insisted."

"You meant well."

There was, I noticed, tenderness in my voice.

"Let's go there," he said.

We sat down in the reception area, just beyond the hotel foyer. We sat on large leather chairs facing out onto the street. A door was open, and with that air and the stream of light flooding through the windows I felt able to bear anything that was to come.

"Francis rang you," I began.

My voice trembled a little. I had to fight back the desire to cry. It was a sudden, overwhelming need as if somehow Francis was dead and I was about to hear that news. I looked at Thomas and he began to talk at once, no doubt sensing my tension.

"Firstly, he is well." He paused for a moment. "He didn't want to explain much. Only that he had to leave everything behind him here in the hotel. That he had to leave without the things he had brought."

"Where are these things?" I asked quietly. I had not asked before.

"The manager has them locked away for us. We can take them whenever we want."

"And Francis really does not want them?"

"He wanted to disappear. He wanted the sensation of disappearing. It was a need." Thomas waved his hand dismissively. "I can't explain why. He can't explain why. I guess it was a sort of buzz he got in breaking with the past like that. He said he knew it would cause us distress, but that on a deeper level he didn't care."

"At least he was honest," I said. My throat felt tight. I knew I would never, ever hold Francis in my arms. I would never kiss him. He had died. In a way, what I had dreaded was a reality. He had killed himself to get away from his old life. He had killed the links that led back to us, and this call to Thomas, I sensed, was one part of the little more he had to offer us.

"Just tell me where he is," I demanded.

"In Paris," Thomas replied.

"But not for long," I added. "I can sense there's more you're finding difficult to say."

Thomas fidgeted. His dark eyes looked around the room as if for outside help. His youth showed itself clearly to me. He had been given a load that was too heavy.

"He is in love," he said at last.

The words hit me like a blow to the chest. I drew in great gulps of the air that was coming in through the door. To breathe. How precious it was to breathe. I wanted an end to coffins. I wanted all the coffins in the world to be destroyed. I wanted death itself to be annihilated. Useless death. Its white empty blaze filled me with despair. The love I felt for Francis was a death too, and now it was linked with these words that he was in love. Life-affirming love, and it was not for me.

"Who is it?" I managed to say.

"He would not tell me her name, only that she is much older than him and understands his needs completely."

"Does she?"

The words were vague. I had nothing more really to add. I wondered what this unknown woman felt, by being able to understand him. Had she touched his bright hair? Had she been able to do that? Was she able to do that anywhere she wanted? The pain ground itself into me. Why don't I break apart now? I thought.

"They are going away together to live. He wouldn't say where. He inferred he did not want us to know."

"And his studies?" I asked.

The stupid question was stupid because it was sensibly practical, and I felt nothing of that. I, in my madness, was not practical.

"You look ill," Thomas said.

"Do I?"

I knew my voice sounded remote. I stared out through the glass at the grey of Paris and the relative boredom of the view on offer. Only the light of the sun was keeping me going, keeping me from that breakdown I both feared and in a way longed for. Why don't I break apart now? The thought was persistent.

"Won't you at least have a drink," Thomas asked. "I could do with some alcohol."

"A glass of wine," I said.

I watched as Thomas got up. I was glad to be alone for a moment. The hammer blows were still hitting at me. Love. The meaningless, beautiful word. As opaque and as impossible to know as death. Then quite suddenly, from another building I heard Schubert's *Piano Trio No. 2*. For the remainder of the time I had before Thomas returned, I listened to the quiet majesty of the music. The hammer blows became less fierce, and I became calmer. When Thomas came back he handed me the wine in silence, and I sipped at it slowly. The outer world brought me beauty of sound, and now this delicate taste of wine. I wanted to know what the wine was, but the question seemed too irrelevant to ask. In fact there was nothing to ask at all. Francis was in love, and I was gazing into a void: a void filled with the comfort of music and the warmth of drink and sun, but a void all the same.

"He wants to meet you, Father."

Again a blow. I wanted to scream that I couldn't. Couldn't. That there was no way I could meet my son now. My reply sounded dry and empty as I said, "When and where?"

"Outside the church of Saint-Séverin at three this afternoon."

"I didn't know Francis liked medieval churches. A strange choice."

"It's better than a bar," Thomas observed.

"Does he want to see both of us?"

Thomas finished the glass of wine and shook his head.

"Only you," he replied. "But if you cannot face it alone, I can wait nearby. There is a place I know on the rue de la Huchette."

"Yes," I said automatically. "I think it would be good to have you nearby."

I glanced at him as I said this. I saw his face brighten. I knew he had wanted me to say yes to his proposal.

"Shall we walk over there together?" he asked. "It is a beautiful day. That is if you think you have rested enough."

"Thomas, I was not here yesterday. I was not shut in my room resting as you put it. I was out there in the Paris streets, and I saw the back of a boy who I thought was Francis. When I ran after him he had gone, disappeared into one of the buildings."

"Perhaps you did see him," he said, "in a dream. Father, you were here. The cleaning woman asked if she could come into the room and you said no. She heard that quite clearly."

"And she told you that?"

"Yes. Is there any reason for her to have lied?"

"I heard sounds from your room before I came down to the breakfast room. That terrible, mechanical voice."

"You see? It's a delusion. Francis –"

He reached out again with his hand and put it on my arm. It was the first time I could recall him using my Christian name.

"Francis," he repeated, "the shock of his disappearance –" He paused. "The shock of it and the rush of coming here to Paris unexpectedly, probably fearing the worst. I know what you are going through."

"And what is the worst?"

"His death of course," he replied, "or a disappearance that could never be resolved."

"But he is going to disappear," I insisted.

"It's not the same. At least you will know he is going with someone he says he loves, and who knows, in time he may return."

"You mean to England?"

"To the house. To you. In time."

I closed my eyes wearily. The music had stopped. I sat listening to the sound of vehicles in the street, and by a distant bridge the calling of a child's voice. It sounded lost, and the sound was bleak.

"Now I will go to my room and take a few hours to get myself ready. I don't mean physically, but mentally. I shall meet you here, Thomas, in this room at one. We can walk there slowly. Is that alright with you?"

"Yes, Francis," Thomas replied and pressed my arm with his hand. I realised his hand had been resting on my arm for quite a long time – long enough to declare affection.

I passed Thomas's room on the way to my own. I listened outside the door. I heard no sounds coming from within. The metallic cries had died, and as I thought of the repetition of the word yes, I wondered if it had been a continuation of my dream. There had been the desperation of love and the parting of death, and in Thomas's room I had heard the terrible yes that goes hand in hand with both. On a sudden impulse I pressed my body against the wood of the door, pressed hard my imprint on the entrance I could not enter.

"Yes," I said as I pressed myself there, but I had no idea to what or to whom.

At one I met Thomas. Although the sun was out the air had grown colder. The grey buildings of Paris shone with a deep golden colour, the burnished yellow that marks the decline of the year. We crossed the Seine, which was at low ebb, and entered the island that holds the Sainte-Chapelle and Notre-Dame. I was tired and wished Francis had arranged to meet me outside one of these. I glanced at the long queue waiting to enter the Sainte-Chapelle and saw an old woman there, leaning heavily on a stick. She looked exhausted, but her face was grim and determined. She had a look that seemed to say, this is the last thing I want to do before I die. I am accomplishing a wish in coming here, in standing here. I will not fail now. I will not collapse.

I imagined her thinking this in the brief glance I had of her, and hurried to catch up with Thomas who was ahead of me.

"Are you alright?" he asked.

"Tired," I said. "I saw an old woman. She was standing

outside the Sainte-Chapelle. There were at least a hundred people in front of her, waiting to get in. But she looked so fixed in her objective, so sure she would make it inside to the chapel, despite her tiredness. I am years younger than her, and I realised my own tiredness was a whim, maybe an evasion. Maybe I do not want to meet Francis after all."

"You don't mean that," Thomas replied flatly.

"No, I don't mean that," I said.

We reached Notre-Dame and crossed the small bridge that divides the island from the left bank. I glanced over at the garden in front of the church of Saint-Julien-le-Pauvre, and Thomas, seeing my look, suggested we sit in the garden for a while.

"Francis may pass by," I said. "He may see us."

Thomas laughed.

"So what? I have a right to accompany you here, even if I don't meet him with you."

We sat in silence in the garden. I shivered a little and drew the light jacket I had chosen to wear closer around me.

"The sun is cooling," Thomas said.

A dog ran up to us barking, and an anxious owner called it away. My mind had gone completely blank. I had no desire left to see Francis, or to hear reasons why or explanations that would either excuse or justify. I felt low on emotion, and yet at the same time as I sat there I restrained myself from bursting into tears. Inside I was being torn apart, yet something within was protecting me from that feeling, giving me a sort of armour: an armour that covered my outward emotions like a thin membrane.

"What time is it?" I asked at last.

"A quarter to three," Thomas replied, looking at his watch.

"I had better go. He may be early."

"Then I will stay here for a while longer," Thomas said. "This is one of my favourite spots in Paris. Then I will go and have a drink in the rue de la Huchette, but by four I will be back here. We can meet here then."

I stood up, looked down at Thomas and nodded my head. He raised his hand in a silent goodbye, and I walked out of the garden and quickly made my way to Saint-Séverin. I saw Francis at once, before he had seen me. He was wearing a well-cut black duffle coat, and I noticed he had a paperback stuffed into one of his pockets. His fair hair blew in the slight breeze, and it contrasted well with the dark clothes he was wearing. From a distance he looked older than his years. He looked as if he was in his mid-twenties. He was walking up and down outside the portal of the church, and I wondered if he was impatient to get this meeting over with. Immediately I felt attracted to him, the thin membrane of my armour broke, and the full force of my emotions for him came rushing to the surface.

"Francis," I called.

He looked up and saw me. There was no smile on his face as he stepped forward to greet me. He had to pass a group of men, tramps who were lying sprawled out in front of the church. One grabbed at his duffle coat with a dirty hand, and I saw with surprise that Francis hit at the hand, pushing it violently away.

"Just a little money," I heard the man say.

Francis reached me, muttering that he had been pestered by these men for a good quarter of an hour.

"You said three," I reminded him.

"Yes," he replied impatiently. "My bloody watch was fast."

"Anyway, we are both here now," I said to pacify, but instead of looking at me, Francis stared at the huddle of men.

"Paris is full of them," he said. "They are a nuisance."

"They are poor," I said simply.

"Most of them need not be on the streets," Francis said glibly. "They are just lazy."

"You know that, do you?" I asked.

"Simone has no patience with them," he added, speaking this woman's name as if she was completely familiar to me.

"Simone is –?"

"Shall we go inside the church?" he asked, not answering my question. "At least they won't let these men in there."

"How Christian of them," I couldn't help but say.

"Father, what do you know about what makes a man poor?"

There was a jeering note in his voice that was unpleasant. A feeling of dislike towards my son came to the surface, along with all the other conflicting emotions.

"Obviously not as much as you," I said sarcastically.

We entered the interior of the church. It was the first time I had been inside since the time I was living in the city so many years ago. The walls were in need of repair and the place looked generally more run-down than I had remembered it. The magnificent forest of columns at the far end of the church still startled me with their mystery and beauty.

"It has been so long," I murmured, "so long since I have been here."

"How long is that?" he asked.

"Since I used to come here to listen to concerts. Before you were born. I was here for a while, you know," I added.

"Oh," he said and left it at that. He was clearly disinterested.

We walked down the centre of the church towards the altar. A stark, rather ugly neon-lit cross stood there.

"Let's sit down," he said.

We sat next to each other and there was a long silence. I waited for him to begin talking. I had no desire to begin myself. There was so much hostility in him I was afraid to be the one to start a conversation. Could we really converse at all? I wondered to myself.

"Thomas told you I rang him," he said at last.

"Of course. Otherwise I would not be here."

"And he told you about Simone?"

"He did not tell me her name, but yes he told me that you had met someone."

"I am in love with her," he said abruptly. There was a

coldness in his voice that appeared a million light years away from loving, or what I called loving.

"And she loves you?" I asked.

"Yes."

Then silence. A long, long silence. He looked moodily around him, ostensibly looking at the stained-glass windows, but I'm not sure whether he wasn't perhaps just killing time, just looking at anything that was there so as not to look at me. Perversely, I decided to tease him.

"The gothic windows are fifteenth century," I began, "I like especially St John the Evangelist – the green, yellow and red with a touch of blue on his cloak. I like especially his glorious yellow hair. His beautiful fair hair."

I knew the church windows off by heart. Long ago I had had a passion for gothic stained-glass, and had come to study them often when I lived in Paris. I had not totally wasted all of my time on painful adventures. Francis remained silently looking. He knew I knew he was observing nothing.

"Simone has promised to teach me everything about Paris churches," he said.

"A sentimental education," I murmured.

"Father, that was a cheap retort," and saying that he turned to look at me.

"Yes, I suppose it was," I replied. "but it seems we have to begin somewhere in talking about this issue."

"Not like that," he said curtly.

"Then how do you want to talk about it?"

"Alright, Father, I'll put it simply. She is older than me. Twenty years older in fact. The age thing makes no difference to me, and it doesn't to her. She wants to take me away from Paris. She has a place in a distant country I don't want to name, and I will live with her there."

"So you won't tell me where you intend to go?"

My voice was now shaking. I felt a sickening feeling in my stomach. I was going to lose him completely and it meant nothing to him. I could tell it meant nothing to him by the chill in his voice, by the empty look in his eyes. The rawness of my intense feelings scratched at my insides and burnt in my brain. I looked briefly at the cross on the altar, but there was no help there. I was alone with my useless, pathetic passion.

"And the rest of your education?" I managed to say.

"Damn all that," he said.

"You may say that now –"

"– and I'll say it later. I want to get as far away as I can with her."

"What is it you especially love in her?" I asked.

Tormenting and tormented words were a struggle to utter. She was an older woman. My age perhaps. The ageless child in me cried out, why not me? Why not me?

"Her knowledge of life is so vast," he said. "I could spend a lifetime learning from her. She wants to teach me everything about the beauty of life and the light in it. She is full of light."

There was a sudden emotion in his voice that had brought him to life. His eyes were no longer empty. They were bright in the gathering gloom of the church.

"And what about later? When time goes by and you are older, and she is older? Do you believe this feeling you have can survive those years?"

I was playing the role of the concerned father now. I was a character in an opera. Maybe the father in *La Traviata* pleading with his son. I was saying words that masked the real feeling that hit at the very core of me, the emotion that said I was in love with my son and that I did not want a woman of almost my own age to replace me.

"I believe my feelings will last," he said.

As he said these words I felt the fervour he had previously exposed towards her draw back, ebb back inside himself. The familiar coldness was returning.

"And where do I come into this?" I asked.

"I don't understand."

"It's not hard to understand. You have a father and a

brother. You intend to go away to a far country with a woman neither of us have either met or know, and you are indifferent, or seem to be indifferent, about that fact."

"Should I be otherwise?" he murmured.

"You mean I suppose that there is no love lost between us."

"Father," he said, "be realistic. You had no time for us as children –"

"And you are barely more than a child now," I interrupted.

"Yes, but unlike you or my brother she can bring me real experiences, real life. She won't shut me up in some dreary house in England or make me pursue studies I am not suited for. She says I will learn what I want to learn, and that she will guide me whenever I need it, but never intrude. She believes in learning with passion what one needs, not what the world expects of you."

"A good theory. No doubt she is rich and can afford to indulge herself and you." I paused, and then hit him with the words, "You know you will be nothing more than a kept boy if you go away with her."

I was in full operatic flow with this thrust, but Francis laughed, laughed in my face, and then looked away from me, trying to control his laughter.

"I don't care about that," he spluttered. His laughter sounded feverish, almost sick in its harsh hilarity, and I knew as I heard him that he really did not care, and that he was oblivious to the fact he would be considered a paid companion.

"What of it?" he added. "What of it, how one has money, as long as one is not poor?"

In my mind's eye I saw him hitting away the hand of the poor man outside of the church.

"And will you marry eventually?" I asked.

"If it makes me secure financially, then yes," he replied. "There may be reasons why it's needed, but we consider ourselves married already."

Equally in my mind I saw him having sex with this

woman. I saw him being taught by her. The positions to take, the pleasure to be found. I vomited, almost literally vomited up the statement, "Then you have had sex."

"It was the first thing we had," he replied with a sort of casual brutality. "It was the first thing we wanted. The rest would not have worked out without it."

"You've had little other experience of sex," I observed.

"I realised in sex you don't – or I don't – need much experience to satisfy," he said.

There was a crudeness in this that made me feel even sicker than I already was. I wanted to rush out of the church. Leave him, and in leaving, leave behind the carnal images I was having of him with this woman.

"Well, you have told me," I said at last.

I glanced around the church as I said these words. I was slipping away into a sickening darkness. Francis made no reply, but just sat there, and as I tried to look at him again I saw he was looking down at his hands. They were twisting together in a gesture that seemed to speak of anguish. I realised there were no bridges to cross to reach my son, to know who he was or how he felt. But there in Saint-Séverin I realised how I felt. I wanted to hold him to me, kiss his hands and then his mouth. I wanted to undo all the learning this woman had supposedly taught him and impose upon him a learning of my own. I wanted above all to be his master, both in body and in mind.

"I suppose the Hemingway I gave you didn't teach you much," I said.

He looked at me in surprise, as if to say, who the hell is Hemingway? He leant back and looked up into the vast high reaches of the church.

"I couldn't read more than the first book," he said. *"The Sun Also Rises."*

He looked back down as he said the title, and then turned to stare at me.

"An impotent war veteran from World War One. A picture

of Paris and boredom, of cafés and mentally deficient men and women. Then there was the bull-fighting in Spain. The killing of horses, and the killing of bulls. Bickering among the men and the women, and then some poor sod of a young bull-fighter who cuts a bull's ear off and gives it to this ghastly stereotyped English woman." He paused, and then said with finality, "It meant nothing to me."

"You should have read the second book," I replied, already defeated.

"Oh, the love story. I dipped into it. Got the gist of it. The woman dies. I remember that. She dies after delivering a still-born child. She's called Catherine." He paused again. "How could I forget her name?" His voice was sharp and cutting as he added, "Catherine has to die, doesn't she? Is that what you meant me to learn from the book?"

Defensively I replied, "It seems you did read *A Farewell to Arms*."

"No, only enough to know the bones of it, but I read the first one in full. There was one sentence in particular I remember. It was about them all seeming to be such nice people."

He laughed again in my face.

"Do you think there were nice people? I had Simone read it and she thought it was a dreadful book, with dreadful people."

"And being in love with her, you value her opinion?"

"I wasn't much good at studying at school, Father, but I can have an opinion that belongs to me alone. But yes, I valued the fact that she agreed with me. Anyway, the books are with the other things in the hotel, stored away somewhere no doubt. Useless to say I don't want any of those things back."

I had had enough. He was slaughtering me, and I was just sitting there and accepting it. And yet, the terrible love I felt for him made me remain where I was. This would perhaps be the last time I would see him for a long time, maybe ever, and

I had to take it all in: the insults open and implicit, the sarcasm and the disinterested coldness that felt like hate.

"You didn't have to disappear from your room as you did," I said. "You made it look as if you had had an accident somewhere. That you had been –"

I stopped, lost for words. Soon I would start to cry if it continued like this.

"As if I had been what?" he asked crisply. "Abducted? Stolen? Murdered? What high drama would you like put on it?"

"Stop it, Francis," I said sharply. "I won't be spoken to like this."

"Sorry, Father," he replied, "I suppose you would like to hear something else from me. But I really don't know what, so you must accept me for at last being myself. Having my own way in my own freedom of saying things."

He edged closer, as if he was mocking me with this closer intimacy. His body was pressed lightly against mine. His face was now very near my face.

"I'll tell you exactly what happened," he said. "I was in the street one afternoon and I saw her on the opposite side. She looked at me at the same time I looked at her. It was in a side street off the boulevard Saint-Germain. I smiled, she smiled and quite suddenly we were together and laughing and suggesting a drink somewhere. We went to Les Deux Magots. We looked for a long time in silence at the sun on the façade of Saint-Germain-des-Prés. I didn't even fully realise we were holding hands until she mentioned that I should go back with her to her house."

He paused, and his face withdrew a little from mine, then came back again as if to renew the attack.

"I liked her house. Full of expensive paintings and very beautiful antique furniture. She's divorced, but that doesn't matter, does it, Father? She is very knowledgeable and rich. She has all I need in a woman. When I said after we had made love that I should return to my hotel, she asked why, and I asked why with her, and we both smiled at the stupidity of it. Of course there was no reason for me ever to go back to that hotel again. Let the things I had there rot. Let anyone take them. She said she would replace everything I had, and the very next day we went shopping and she bought me all the clothes I needed and more."

"More what?" I murmured and moved away from him. I had to have distance from his words, from the smell of his breath on my face. He was a part of me, and he was crucifying me in the church with his words.

"I disappeared because I disappeared."

I closed my eyes. Tears were stinging behind them. He was a part of me, and I did not love him, but I was in love with him. The reality of it plunged me into a hell that was worse than any pulpit description. It was made up of broken bodies and breath that burnt like flames, and a sort of devil sitting in the middle of it, screaming out, love one another, love one another, even if it tears and tears at the soul, even if it burns the skeleton of the soul. Let nothing remain.

"Is there anything else I need say about why I didn't return?" he asked.

He had moved away from me. He suddenly appeared different, like the teenager I had last seen in England. In the fading light of the church I saw again the youth I had visited in his room. I saw in memory him turn away to undress, and then once more I saw the beauty of his buttocks. I was his father and his expectant lover. The young man who had so repulsively breathed upon my face had been transformed by memory into all I desired, into all I wanted to desire.

"Francis," I said simply, and then I fell silent.

He got up and began to walk around the church. He stared up at various windows, and then moved on. I followed him. The absurd notion came into my head that with a little care and discretion I could reclaim him as my son. I began by narrating the subject matter of each window. He said nothing in return, appearing to be listening to what I was saying.

Anybody seeing this from the outside would have thought I was a considerate father, showing off and sharing his knowledge of the stained-glass windows in Saint-Séverin.

But then it was over. The sharp laughter burst any fantasy I had of return. He turned on me in mid-sentence and said, "When is this laughable comedy going to end?"

I stood in silence looking at him. I was lost.

"You're not going to capture me," he said. His voice sounded vicious and high. "I don't know what you feel for me, and I don't want to know. If I really knew, then I would think of you as a monster. I am sure of that."

He stopped talking for a moment, and his face looked ghostly in the dark part of the church where we were standing. Then he resumed talking.

"I would become a monster myself if I was forced to be near you, in the same house with you. With Simone there is light. With you there is only the dark."

I reached out suddenly and caressed his cheek. I had nothing to lose now, and had to touch him. At the moment of contact he shrank backwards from me. I made a move towards him.

"Don't come any nearer," he said.

It was a cold order, and I remained where I was. I had a vision of him disappearing in the forest of the entwined columns, of being taken away, of him wanting to be taken away.

"I want to say –"

"Nothing," he said. "I don't want you, and I don't want to hear anything more from you."

"I love you," I cried, and in that instant I felt shame. Just behind me a priest hurried by. I heard the quiet patter of his shoes and thought, he heard. He heard me make this declaration.

"It's a lie," Francis replied. The whispered force of the reply seemed to echo around me, seemed to echo around the dizzying, swirling forms of the tree-like columns.

"Let's go out into the street," I said.

Again I could hear the priest moving behind us.

"I'll go out into the street. Alone. You stay here and join the holy brotherhood. That's what you should have done years ago, before you met and ruined my mother's life. It would have suited you, that life, with all its secret, dirty I-love-yous."

"Be quiet, Francis," I said. "We are not alone."

"Goodbye, Father."

He spat out the last word mockingly. In a moment he had made it to the entrance door and then he was gone. I sat and put my head in my hands. I felt an overwhelming sense of loss, and at the same time relief. Then I felt a presence behind me, and turning I saw the priest looking down at me.

"Is there anything I can do?" he asked me.

"I don't think so, Father," I said.

"You have had an argument in the house of God," he said quietly. "There was a darkness here until that young man left. I am available if you want to talk about it."

"I'm not sure I can expect your understanding," I replied.

The priest sat next to me. He was a young man, and he had an open, clear face. I felt he knew everything, and at the same time that he knew nothing. I didn't want to soil him with my words or with my thoughts.

"There is nothing good in the relationship you have just had a glimpse of," I said. "Not in your terms anyway."

"And what are my terms?" he retorted simply.

His voice was low and soft, and I had a desire to confess to him how much I was in love with my son.

"I don't want to take anything away," I said. This sounded obscure, so I tried to make myself clearer. "I don't want to take anything away from you, as a person I mean. Talking about my feelings is not for a person like you to hear."

"God can take away," he said. "Not man. Certainly not you. I am hear to listen when men and women are in trouble. I sense you are in trouble."

"I am in love with that boy," I said.

I looked quickly at him to get his reaction, but his face was impassive.

"Is it a good love?" he asked.

"No," I said, "yet I want it."

"How much pain does it give you to want this?"

I looked at him again, but he was staring ahead at the altar. He appeared focused and concentrated: totally there for me, yet at the same time distant enough to give me freedom.

"I feel as if I am in hell," I murmured.

"Hell comes after death if we put ourselves there," he said. "In life we always have a choice, even to the last."

"I would like to believe that," I said.

"Then why don't you?"

"The hell within me prevents it," I said.

"Then try to understand it as being an illusion. A terrible illusion, but one that after a long struggle you can escape from. So many men, even saints have been tortured by this delusion. Prayer is there, and my advice is to pray and to believe you can release yourself from these feelings you call hell."

"Father," I said, "do you know once I too wanted to become a member of the church?"

He turned to me then and smiled.

"The past is as much within us as the present. Can't you find it within you to take the path back? I'm not suggesting to enter the church, but to enter that other church. The church that is always within us and that is always open to welcome us back."

I did not reply. I closed my eyes, and he remained beside me. I tried to visualise a path that would take me away from the hellish world I had created within, but I knew deeply and profoundly I would never be able to find it again. Yet the priest's words had calmed me. The storm was passing. I felt quiet. In this place of inner quietness I saw myself alone in a walled garden, and in one of the walls an old wooden door.

The door opened and Thomas came into the garden to join me. With his entrance I felt troubled and my body began to shake. I opened my eyes.

"Are you ill?"

The young priest looked concerned. With a light hand, he reached out and touched my arm.

"I fear to hope."

I had no idea where these words came from. I tried to get up, but an attack of giddiness made me fall back. I heard as if from a great distance the priest ask me if I wanted some water.

"I don't want to trouble you," I replied.

Even sitting down, the giddiness continued.

"It is no trouble."

I sat without moving until he returned. I drank the water he brought to me.

"I was in a walled garden," I said slowly. "It was a good place until he came into it."

"Do you mean the young man who was here?"

"No," I said, "my other son. I have two sons. One is dark. One is fair. It is the fair one I am in love with, but intuition tells me the dark one will pursue me; pursue me however much I may want to protect myself."

The priest was silent. He looked me in the eyes, and I saw a look of sorrow there; a look that said he was no longer able to help. With great effort I managed to stand. He remained seated.

"I must go," I said.

He smiled up at me. He nodded his head in silence, and then turned his face away. The thought at once imprinted itself on my mind that God does not, can never, ever love his son sexually. It is the only sin God could ever have, but being all good, that he has never possessed.

I walked away from the priest, and as I reached the entrance I turned to look at him one last time. The space where he had been was empty. It seemed to me that he had never been there, or if he had, it had been in a form that I could no longer recognise.

Thomas was in the garden waiting. He must have seen the stricken look on my face for he said nothing. Quietly, I asked him to take me back to the hotel.

"I can bear no more," I said.

Getting up from where he was sitting he took me by the arm and led me out of the garden.

Once back in the hotel I went to my room. I slept almost immediately. I dreamt I had returned to the house (In England? I did not know) but it was boarded up. I was told it would only be habitable if I completely renovated the interior. Once inside I found mould on the walls, and the rooms were empty of furniture.

I was told that the work on the house was difficult but it could be done. I walked from room to room, and felt more and more a dreadful sense of loss. I had lost everything that had once been there: all companionship, all love, all contact with others. I stood at an upstairs window and gazed out over a dark sea I knew had not been there before. It stretched before me. Its dark blue meeting the dark blue of a threatening sky. The sky made me feel a sensation of anguish. I stood back unable to look at it, and for a moment my whole being seemed to close itself off, break down. I knew I had died. It was all gone: the house, a sense of place, my memories, all disappearing into a black centre that encased me totally. I gasped, cried out, then awoke from death, and once more I was at the window, staring out at the ominous sea. The waves lapped with dreadful steadiness on the shore, timeless in their too perfect repetition.

What sea is this? I questioned, but all presence was gone. I would never be told anything again. I was completely single, a rigid statue of a self, staring out at this sea. Then in the near distance, in the heart of the water, a sudden explosion broke the silence. A white light tore the sky and sea apart, ripping the deathly stillness into a yet more terrible stillness. I had been brought back to life to witness the total end of the world. I saw, through the burning aftermath, figures of men and women on the shore, stretching out with useless hands, blinded in their eyes, yet still reaching out for escape. I fell back into the room, realising with horror I had seen the eternity that is the end of all being. Then with an abrupt click of motion I was sitting up in my bed. I was wide awake, brutally awake in the hotel room. Automatically, I switched on some music and then lay back between the sheets. A rush of sexual excitement, a desperation of sexual excitement disturbed me. I pushed the sheets away and lay exposed and naked. I lay as if washed up with all the other dead horrors of my dream. The mockery of it, exposed and naked, listening to the radio in my room. Relief and grief at having survived the dream, reaching down and touching my penis. My penis throbbing to the mournful, ecstatic sound of the final scene of *Tristan und Isolde*. The hammering desire, lifting desire out of death, and then driving it back, deep, deep into the heart of nothingness. The dark edges of nothingness as I pounded at my flesh, conjuring in my mind the image of Francis running from the church. Running from all he sensed in my desire, and I, in the rhythmic humping of my penis, in time to the desolation of Isolde over the body of Tristan, running mentally to catch his escaping form, to clasp him again as the music clasps its love in death, to hold again the strands of blond hair, to caress the cheek of his face an instant only as the music thrashed against my body, submerging me in a compulsive need to calm the heat and cool the flesh.

"Francis," I murmured, and the music reached its peak, folded back into itself and then folded me tightly, very tightly into orgasm. The searing voice on the radio sang, rising out of the orchestra, rising out of finality itself. I did not understand the words, I did not understand in full what they meant, but I heard the call and rose upwards myself. I tried to rise with the last farewell, to leave the last white of sperm in the bed. Tristan was no more (was Francis?) but I too wanted to go: to rise up and out of myself into that terminal, yet so tenderly desired state.

It was both a mockery and a fulfilment. I had spent myself empty to the image of my son. I had voided the void itself, scooping out of myself the very same fluid that had created him. I had given the night the gift of a dying procreation, and in the sheets of the bed a dead infant of impossible life glistened and shone brightly white as it congealed and died.

Tristan.

I heard in the closing sounds of the voice a name given to this fluid from my body and this mockery of a child.

I left the bed. I left the waste of myself behind. I went into the bathroom and stood underneath the shower, letting the hot water pour over my body. I scrubbed at my genitals, scrubbed hard at any remains that were left of my sperm. I towelled myself dry and putting on my clothes, left the room. I went down in the lift to the reception and asked for the manager. I told him who I was, and that I wanted the key to whatever place he had packed away my son's things. I went to a dark room with no windows, only a stark, over-bright, overhead light. I was shown where Francis's things were, and then I was left alone with them. The things he had had that day (what day? What day was it exactly? I had never asked, and I was never told) were neatly piled up. I knelt on the floor and methodically went through his belongings. I separated off the clothes first, discarding them. They were the clothes worn by a boy he no longer was, and they had no meaning now. I held a shirt of his to my face and tried to breathe in his smell, but only smelt the anonymity of an unused article of clothing. He had never worn the shirt. I threw it aside. I disregarded the remainder of the clothes, mentally throwing them all away. Other than clothes there were relatively few other things. The usual sundry toiletries and an eau de cologne I did not remember from England. To my knowledge he had never worn eau de cologne. I unscrewed the top of the bottle and smelt the scent. It was a bitter smell, and it made me feel sick in my stomach. It was not a smell I could associate with Francis. Had some other woman bought it for him? Had he left it behind because he knew very well that Simone would replace it? I put all the articles of the bathroom with the clothes, to be thrown away with the rest of the trivia. But what was not trivia? I found a decided lack of anything I could call personal. There were of course the two Hemingways I had given him, but apart from these there were no other books. A few fashion magazines, and a magazine about cars. I threw the two books and the magazines onto the rest of the stuff. There was nothing else to see, nothing else at all. Then just as I was about to get up off my knees and go I saw part of a photograph peeking out of a jacket. I pulled it out and saw a photograph of Catherine, his mother. It was a smiling close-up of her standing outside a house I could no longer remember. She was holding a white rose, looking directly into the camera. The smile was not false, and the look was one of happiness. I could not remember if I had taken this photograph, and after a little while concluded it had been taken before she had met me. I tried to imagine who the photographer could have been. The bright smile was welcoming, loving, and the way she held the rose forward in her hand seemed to mean something. Had it been plucked for her? Had she taken it from the hand of someone else who loved her, who wanted her? I looked intently at the photo some more, but it retained its mysteries and it always would. I put it into my own jacket pocket, intending to give it to Thomas. I had no idea if he even had a photograph of his mother. Clearly Francis, in his haste to leave everything in the hotel behind him, had forgotten this one unique article, and I had no way of returning it to him now. Even if he discovered its loss I knew he would not come to find it. I closed the door of the room and on returning to the reception told the manager I wanted the things he had stored thrown away.

"But does not Monsieur want anything?"

His voice was crisp and dry. He did not care either way. He

was going through the procedure of care.

"No," I replied with an artificial smile on my face. "My son has gone far away and he will not need these things."

"I hope nothing bad has happened."

The statement was a statement, and in its cold delivery did not ask anything back. I walked away without answering, just giving a vague wave of my hand as I turned from him. Then I saw Thomas standing in the entrance of the hotel. He looked as if he had been out.

"Thomas," I called and went up to him. He asked if I had rested. "I slept," I said.

"Good."

"Have you been out?"

"I walked."

"Where did you walk to?"

My voice sounded mechanical, but despite that I was interested. I wanted to know where he had been.

"I walked to the rue de Rivoli and then into the Tuileries."

I nodded my head approvingly. I looked like a father who was having a pleasant conversation with his son.

"It's a long time since I have been in the Tuileries," I replied. "When I lived here I used to have tea quite often in one of the garden cafés, especially on warm days." I laughed at the banality of my own statement. "I liked the statues. I wonder if they are all still here. Things have changed so much."

"Father," Thomas asked quietly, "are you really alright?"

"Yes. I slept. I needed it." Then I paused and said simply, "It was a tough encounter."

"With Francis?"

"Yes."

Thomas sighed, and I knew he didn't know what to say. He looked awkwardly down at his shoes.

"You too must be tired," I said.

"Oh no." He smiled and looked at me directly in the face as he did so.

"I want to hear more," he added. "I want to hear what he said to you, but perhaps not now."

"You are right. It wouldn't be good to go into it all now. All I can say is he has gone, and I have just looked through the things he left behind in the hotel."

"And?" he asked.

"Nothing. I found nothing."

Then I remembered the photo of his mother, but I couldn't mention it now I had said I found nothing. I tapped my jacket pocket and felt the slight wrinkle of the photo pressing against my breast. I said to myself, almost with an inward hatred, that I might not give it to Thomas at all, that I might throw the photo away with the rest of Francis's things.

Thomas touched my arm. The gesture was spontaneous and caring.

"I think we should go out again," he said. "I know we're tired, but there is nothing to stay in this hotel for. In a way it's all over, isn't it?"

"What?" I asked.

"Searching for Francis. He is found, and as you have just said, gone. There is not a lot left to do in Paris except perhaps to enjoy it a little together before we leave it."

I searched his face for a moment before answering, and then said, "Is that what you want to do?"

"I think it would be good," he replied simply. "You are dressed to go out, and clearly I am. Why stay here?"

His lightness of touch was infectious. The lightness of touch on my arm and the tone of his voice. Both combined strangely to lift me out of the state of morbid excitement I had been in. I was not alone. I had him, Thomas, and he wanted to be with me, to go out with me. I felt a rush of excitement at the thought of spending an evening in Paris with him.

"Where shall we go?" I asked.

"Let's just go," he said.

We crossed Paris in a sort of dizzying silence. I passed from mood to mood: utter despair at the loss of Francis, and then euphoria at being close to this other boy: my other boy. My dark brown boy. We wandered down from the Gare du Nord, criss-crossing streets, passing grey buildings dying in the last muted colours of the passing of the day. It was night when we reached Forum des Halles, and stopped by the fountain on the Place des Innocents that was a focal point when I frequented Café Costes in the eighties. I watched a group of students, around Thomas's age, sitting on the edge of the fountain, splashing water at each other. A new generation, I thought, not my Aids-conscious generation, but a new generation, full of new ideas I had very little knowledge of. I stood still and watched them, and Thomas, intrigued by this, asked me what I was so interested in. I explained slowly, "They are all new, aren't they? They are made from different colours from when I was their age. But you," I added, "you must recognise something in them. Something – some fresh colour you can identify with. You are all painted new, and there must be something there to hold onto."

He laughed softly as I said this, and his laugh had nothing malicious in it, nothing mocking, unlike my other son, my other lost son who would have growled his angry laughter in my face. He said he really did not have much in common with them. In a sense that I perhaps would not understand, he was not cut from the same cloth as them.

"Nor do I perhaps clothe myself in the same colours," he added.

I smiled back at him, wondering at this response, but I said nothing more. We moved on, away from the children of his generation.

We walked to Beaubourg and the square in front of it, that sloping, elongated, modern square in front of the late twentieth century's high capital of art – its cathedral to the peak of our then secure western culture. A few jugglers were performing for a listless crowd, and half hidden within the entrances of the buildings around the square I saw those who were homeless make their beds for the night. I touched

Thomas gently, urging him in silence with a gesture of my other hand to look at one poor old man who was wrapping himself in newspapers and covering himself in a tattered rug. He nodded silently in response, and then motioned to me with his head to look at another building. In the entrance, a young girl no more than fourteen, perhaps less, was bedding herself down in a makeshift shelter made out of cardboard. I asked Thomas if he had seen many teenagers like this in Paris, and he answered yes, and even more in Barcelona. He said this was the future for a great many of his generation.

"Many of my peers will know this and suffer this first hand," he added, "and still we will not have the courage to fight back, to fight back against those who so mercilessly drive us here onto the pavements to sleep, and then into the gutters."

"But aren't you angry?" I replied. "Aren't you angry at my own generation and those who came before me who have brought people of your age to this state? Is there no crusade you can begin or join to end it? Surely your anger can be the impetus?"

"I am angry," he said, "and yet with all the social networks I have at my disposal I still feel alone, powerless. We communicate, but we do not discuss enough face to face. We live in a Babel of solitude. Those in power use it more than we do and speak to each other more than we do. They know how to use the new media as much as we, if not more, and have more spontaneous encounters face to face. Unlike us, they have mastered all the languages of this century, and in that knowledge they have an advantage. They can defeat our anger with a multitude of different means that are out of our control." I asked when he had first noticed this. "Only recently," he replied, "since I left England. Since I have been in Spain and now in Paris. I can see there is a need for a great overwhelming revolt, but equally I feel that unlike those who have risen up in the Middle East, we lack passion. We lack the sheer force of numbers who are willing to take on the systems we live under." He smiled shyly at me and murmured, "It is all new to me. The poverty I was protected from is all new to me." Then he continued, "I wonder if Francis has seen it? The poverty around him? Poverty full stop?"

To this I replied, "Yes, I think he has seen it."

I wanted to add that I had seen him physically hit out at it, had seen him openly reject those who were dispossessed outside of Saint-Séverin. But I could not betray him. Whatever Thomas felt about his brother, I could not hold up this contrast of response. The light boy, dark in his vision of what was happening around him. While he, Thomas, the dark one, was so vivid with inner light in his response.

"Take her some money," I said and handed him some notes. "While you take this money to the girl I will take the same to the old man."

Thomas moved away to the building entrance where the teenage girl had made her bed. I went to the old man. He was about to go to sleep, nestling into the papers, wrapped tight in his rug. He noticed me coming, his eyes still alert to danger and he looked up at me with pale, defeated eyes. I put the money down beside him, and a weary hand moved out from its cover to take it inside. He muttered up at me, "Thank you, thank you, but this is not enough. It is not enough to keep me alive."

I asked him what more I could do. He replied, "I am losing my sight. Soon I will be blind, and then I will be a target for any thug who wants to abuse me and eventually kill me." Then he repeated, "But thank you, Monsieur. Believe me, I am grateful that you singled me out from all the others. You did as much as you could do."

He looked up at me, opening wide a mouth void of teeth, and smiling, put his head to rest on his pillow of stone. As I stepped back I began to shiver, and felt I would fall down, pass out there on the pavement in front of him. I saw Francis, my son, in the beggar. I saw how he could be; how in a distant future where I would no longer exist, he would be. I saw him alone on a hard, rocky shore. Wearing rags, and despite the heat of an alien, southern land, cold. Separate and cold, yet still fragilely clinging on to the world. The image clung to my eyes and made them burn with pain. I cried out, and as I cried out I felt myself held and then held even more tightly in strong arms. I was now openly sobbing in Thomas's arms.

"I saw Francis in the future," I said, tears and mucus mingling on my lips as I spoke. He said it was a waking nightmare, that Francis would never end like that. That he was not made to meet such an end. But still I sobbed and held Thomas tightly to me. I heard myself saying, "It must not happen to you. You must not let life drive you insane. You must not let the terrible streets of man capture you."

I realised I was being incoherent, but as I sobbed and spoke I still saw the fair boy who I loved transformed into an older man, and then an old man. I saw him balding, then bald, with teeth, and then without teeth. I saw the death of any hope dry up within him, and watched in my mind's eye as he fell down in need of food and shelter in an unwelcoming land.

"She will take him there," I said. "Simone will drag it all out of him. Drag out his hope and his last innocence, sucking him into an emptiness of useless wandering. She will make him a stranger on the earth, and then when he eventually wants to come home he will find –"

I stopped. I stopped talking, and I ceased to sob. It was ugly being in this pathetic state of despair. I pushed Thomas away and wiped my face with the back of my hand. Thomas forced tissues on me and I blew my nose, and then I shook my head. I said I was strung out by what had happened that day, that I was an idiot and a fool and I could not inflict this ugly sight on Thomas. I felt his tenderness as he led me from the square, away from Beaubourg, to the terrace seats of a café in a street nearby. There were not many people seated there, and I sat in a far corner, as close to the dark as I could get. I watched as Thomas went to fetch a waiter, saying as he went that he would bring me what I needed. When he returned he had a glass of brandy, and almost like a nurse, forced me to drink it down. I felt a rush of relief as the hot liquid entered my throat. The giddiness returned at the shock of the alcohol on an empty stomach, but I did not care anymore. If I passed out now, I would be safe in the arms of my second son. But as I thought this an inner voice said, *You fraud, you ridiculous fraud. Who do you think you are? Some new St. Francis of Assisi in the square in front of one of our modern cathedrals, taking off all your mental clothes? Do you think you can get away with displaying your fraudulent self in its modern incarnation of despair and giving generously to the poor? It is profoundly insane, and you know it. You are too poor in spirit to care for the poor in flesh. Your spiritual poverty has thinned your soul. You have no inner flesh left to help others. You are empty. A walking emptiness that still believes it is alive, still believes it has the right to exist. Well, listen. You are dead. You died when your sperm covered the bed with your white death in the hotel room. There is nothing true or valid you can do, least of all to show off to your other son that you care for the welfare of others. There is no welfare for others in your private hell.*

"What are you saying?"

I heard Thomas talk to me. Had I spoken aloud? The fraudulent St. Francis covered his nakedness with the only inner clothes he could find.

"It is the shock," I replied. "The shock of the drink. It has made me aware of what I have lost in myself in this city."

"We all lose in the cities," he said. "All cities take from us."

"What do you mean?" I asked.

"In my room in England I wondered about going to Barcelona. It was a safe choice. It was not my first choice."

"And what was your first choice?"

At that moment the waiter came and placed another brandy in front of me. In front of Thomas he placed a full bottle of wine.

"Do you intend to get us drunk?" I asked.

The inner voice within replied, *Yes, go on. Blind what you see about yourself with drinks. Forget all that you know.* And as the inner voice ceased I heard a rush of elation in my outer voice as it said again, "Thomas, do you intend to get us drunk?"

He said nothing in reply, but smiled and poured himself a glass of wine, then downed it in one go. He looked across at me and said, "Come on, drink up that brandy. I ordered a third to arrive when you have finished that one."

"First tell me what your choice was other than Barcelona?"

"It was about going to Romania," he said. "I had read about the mountains there, the wild mountains filled with animals of all kinds. I dreamt of discovering a plain at the top of one of those mountains: a plateau where I would find the boys who had been transformed into stags."

"What?" I asked, sensing the wildness in Thomas's voice. I wanted very much to hear about his dream, to hear about his fantasy.

"The boys who had disobeyed their fathers," he said, "and had become stags – transformed into animal form, roaming together in the high forests, then on to the secret plateau."

He paused as if he was dazed by what he was saying. I looked at his face, at his eyes. His eyes shone with a brightness I had never seen before. There was a madness there, a passion that made me want to hear more, and yet scared to hear more.

"Go on," I said.

"Then the fathers came hunting with guns," he replied, "and in the firing of the guns, did not recognise, or perhaps recognised too much that they were killing their sons."

I drank down the brandy. Again I felt it burn. I looked at my dark son and saw a similar madness to my own. Would he kill me or would I kill him? How could I tell him that in the story the boys also had guns? They had disobeyed their fathers and gone up into the mountains to kill the stags wantonly, and it was the mountains themselves that had taken a primal revenge by transforming them into stags? Transforming them so their fathers would come with guns, and either on purpose or unknowingly would kill them? I saw within myself the high plateau empty of trees and the stags' sons exposed to the guns. I too had heard this strange story, literally heard it in a cantata by Béla Bartók. There was a hard, bitter core, an ambiguity in its meaning I did not understand, and still do not understand. But I did understand the dark impulse of torment that could exist between father and son, and the realisation that it had always been and would continue to be until the end of time. And yet, hadn't I tried in my own transgressive way to break it in my physical desire for Francis? I saw again in my drunken state the smoke of gunfire and the dead sons falling to their death. I saw Francis falling to his own death in a far distant land, and what of Thomas? Again I said to myself, would he kill me or would I kill him?

"Perhaps the story is not completely right," Thomas said. "Maybe the fathers did not kill their sons after all." He interrupted my twisting, haunted thoughts with this statement.

"You tell it very well. You have made it your own. Made it exactly as I made it long ago. I prefer this story."

"But I did dream about this hidden, secret place," he continued. "I wished to find it, to see it for myself. But then how could I find somewhere that only exists in myth?"

"It exists somewhere in the collective mind," I replied. "I was young like you when I heard Bartók use it as a basis for a piece of music. Perhaps it is a story a lot of young men know. Especially those who want to leave their homes."

He gave me a piercing look with his eyes as I said this. It had the red core of the darkness of the gun in it. I fell back into the shadows, trying to hide from him. I closed my own eyes for a while and listened to his voice.

"So I chose Barcelona. I chose a place that had mystery for me, but not an impossible place of the imagination. Who knows?" He laughed. "Maybe I would have found something like the boys' plateau if I had gone to Romania." Then he looked at me and observed, "Aside from what has happened with Francis, you seem disoriented by this city, like the Japanese who sometimes fall ill because of the coldness here, the lack of friendliness and manners. It is not as they portray it in sentimental films, nor is there that classical order portrayed in the best of French literature, although it does exist on the level of their architecture, but that too could be considered cold and often grey and forbidding."

I opened my eyes.

"I hadn't thought about it like that," I replied.

My mind was exhausted, and his observation was frighteningly real and yet foreign to me. I heard the sound of someone approaching the table. The waiter returned with the third brandy. I watched as the man put it in front of me. I had a sudden urge to escape the terrace table where I felt mysteriously trapped: to go to a toilet in the café, to lock myself for a while in a place of safety. I moved my legs in an attempt to stand, but they felt weak. I realised I would not be able to stand without Thomas's help, and I was afraid of his help. I saw him as a gaoler keeping me prisoner at the table. My mind was dizzy with this brutal thought, and yet with the thought came an unexpected passion. I needed Thomas. I needed his madness to meet mine. I needed him to hold me in his arms, and yes, if it had to be, to kill me in this open public place. Kill me with a crushing force I could not resist. The image of him squeezing the breath out of my body gave my body an immediate physical reaction. Like the hanged man is supposed to feel at the moment of execution, I felt the hardness of an erection growing in my groin. Was I to spill again my dead seed? This time for the desire of my second son?

"But you must have found something in Barcelona," I said hurriedly, both wanting to escape and yet wanting to know more. I was struggling for breath. He drew forward and then across the table, and looked at me for what seemed a long time before answering.

"Yes," he replied. "It was not something, it was someone. His name was Luis. He was dark like me, and passionate in a different way than anything I had imagined, I was transformed. The boy that I was, was transformed. Like a stag. Yes, like that, except in human form. A stag that has left its home far behind. Yet despite this illusory freedom I was not able to love him."

Hearing these words, these confessional words, a cry went up inside me. He is like me, I thought, he is like me. We are not father and son only, but brothers as well. Brothers of a different generation. Our sex responds to the same stimulus, to the same needs. I looked across the table at him, but his head was down. I reached out then and clasped his hand.

"I am out of shape," I said. "Two brandies, a third waiting, and I already feel drunk, or is it the effect of the words you have just spoken?"

He lifted his head and stared at me. There was a smile on his face. I imagined I was seeing the smile of a wild beast, suddenly tamed. He will not kill me yet, I said to myself and drank down the third brandy. Thomas followed my every move with his eyes, and the smile still played around his lips. What creature are you? I whispered to myself. What is the real intention behind you revealing your secret self to me?

"I'm happy you experienced this relationship in Barcelona," I said, "and it is partly this drink you have given me that makes me capable of saying it, saying it without reservations. But I do have to ask you one question."

"What?"

He leaned even closer towards me. I could feel his eager breath on my face. He opened his mouth slightly, and I saw his white teeth glisten. There was also the tantalising glimpse of his saliva. In my own mouth I tasted blood.

"Was it what you really needed, really desired, this experience . you had? Was it at the heart of your journey?"

"At the heart? Of course it was at the heart of it."

He cried out these words, and I knew then that he was made in my image. That he had come truly from my flesh.

"Luis."

I said the other boy's name. I had said the name of his lover. I wanted to taste the name of the boy that was somehow mixed in with the burst of blood in my mouth.

"Did you really not love Luis?" I asked.

"At first I thought yes," he replied, "but no, I wanted something else. I cannot tell you yet what that something else was. Still is."

"A woman?" I asked.

"No," he said. "I do not find women attractive. I do not want them as lovers. Maybe I have always known I didn't, and that was partly what separated me from my brother."

"When I was your age I felt like you. I was as real in my response to another man as you say you are. I was not in love either, but it was what I wanted."

"You were not like me," he said. His eyes blazed for a moment as if from anger. "You turned away from men to women. You met my mother, and were there not other women before her?"

"It was not a true marriage," I said.

The blood now tasted very bitter, and I swallowed again and again to get rid of the acrid taste. Thomas was forcing me to confess. I knew he would not free me until I had told him all of the truth.

"I went against my own nature to get married," I said. "I crucified a woman by marrying her. I gave myself to her only to have children, to have a son above all."

"Francis," he said flatly.

"I have no preference. I have two sons." I paused. "Is it cruel of me to say that going through that marriage was worthwhile for that?"

"She is in her grave," he murmured. "She released you from what you did not want. She released you from her body."

"I was cruel," I said.

The blood in my throat and in my stomach was making me feel sick. I had to stop now. I had to stop remembering Catherine.

"Please get me another brandy," I said. "The taste is bitter."

"What taste?"

"No matter. Just get me a drink."

He got up from the table and went into the café. A beggar came to the table and held out his hand for money. He was a young man, perhaps a few years older than Thomas. His youthful hand was black with dirt. I placed all the coins I had in his hand, and with a nod of his head he went away. St. Francis of the damned, I thought to myself as Thomas returned with the brandy. As I began to drink it down he poured himself another large glass of wine.

"Has the taste gone?" he asked.

"Yes," I lied. "It has gone."

I watched as he waved at the waiter to come over. He ordered more brandy for me.

"No more," I said.

"I want you drunk, Father. Tonight I want you so drunk you will forget that we are your sons. Above all I want you to forget Francis."

"No more," I repeated. "No more brandy."

But Thomas was relentless. He ordered yet another brandy, and watched fiercely over me until I had drunk it down. This was my fifth, and soon we were both drunk, totally drunk and laughing. What we were laughing about I do not know and cannot remember. We laughed so loudly that the few other people on the terrace turned to stare at us.

"We are creating a scandal," I said.

"To hell with them," he replied.

"Yes, to hell with them," I added. "We are living up to our reputation of being English."

"Exactly."

"Exactly."

But even as we laughed, I knew it sounded hollow even to ourselves. Somehow both of us had confessed ourselves out, or almost, for there were still things we were holding back. The darkness in him was too full of secrets and hidden desires to be confessed in one go. He was an extension of my own guilty flesh, so how could it be otherwise? I sensed he was, like me, capable of cruelties. I wondered what he had inflicted on Luis in Barcelona.

"I will never marry," he said at last as we stumbled away from the table. It was closing time.

"Never?" I asked.

"I have too strong a desire for something that is impossible," he admitted enigmatically.

I did not ask him what, and for the rest of the night we wandered the streets of Paris. We walked the length of the rue de Rivoli, past Concorde and up to the top of the Champs-Elysées. He seemed now to be enjoying himself, and he talked constantly: of books he had read, of buildings he had liked in Barcelona. He did not talk of feelings, but of what he had read and seen, and wanted to share with me. The effect of all that we had drunk was still strong in us, but he was lucid, and to share with him I talked about the books I had read and some of the places I had seen in my own youth. Towards dawn, we approached the Gare du Nord and the area of our hotel. As we approached the street that led to it I suddenly burst out with the words, "He was a bastard to go missing like that: to disappear and make me afraid."

Thomas looked at me, and there was a harsh tone in his voice as he replied, "Like one of the Romanian boys who went up into the mountains to shoot at stags and got transformed."

"Do you think she has transformed him?"

We crossed a bridge over the tracks of the Gare de l'Est. An early train gathered speed beneath us. Our hotel was a few steps away.

"The woman?" he asked.

"Yes, the woman," I said in total complicity with his tone of contempt.

"To hell with it," he concluded.

We went into the foyer of the hotel and sat down on a small sofa facing the reception desk. There was no one there. Perhaps the person who should have been there was sleeping. It was an hour or so before breakfast.

"Maybe we should wait up to eat something," I said.

"Not a thing for me," he replied. "I would like another drink though. It's a pity those machines that hold soft drinks and chocolate don't have alcohol for the needy."

"For alcoholics." I laughed.

"Are we that?"

"You're too young to be an alcoholic," I said back. "It takes time and practice to become an alcoholic."

"Clearly you have not looked closely at people of my generation in England," he replied. Then he went over to the machine holding the soft drinks and chocolate and did a silent pantomime act of kicking it on with his feet.

"Stop pretending to be a child," I said, still laughing at his antics. He looked delightful to me, mimicking being a thug.

"I am a child, Father," he said with sudden seriousness. He came then and sat next to me.

"A drunk too," he added.

"Don't say that word," I said softly.

"Drunk?"

"Father."

"Oh," he said, and laughed.

The laugh was deep and strong, and I knew it was mocking me.

"Don't you want me to be your son?"

His voice was slurred. I sensed the nastiness in his voice of a drunk who knows it is impossible to get another drink.

"I just want you to be Thomas. The Thomas who thought himself equal enough, friend enough to tell me the truth about himself."

"That I am gay?"

"That you like men, yes."

Suddenly there was an uneasy silence between us. He was sobering up rapidly. Soon he would be looking at himself and at me clearly, and I was afraid of what he might see. I didn't have to wait very long before he said, "The last time I saw you before Paris I was barely more than a child. Well, I'm not a child any longer. I have fucked a man since then. That makes me a man, doesn't it?"

He looked at me with a sharp sideways look. I attempted to stand up, but he pushed me back onto the sofa.

"Don't walk away from me when I want to talk to you," he said. "Fuck this place for not having alcohol."

"We have to sober up sometime," I said.

"But not yet," he replied, "not yet."

"We need sleep. We can talk later."

"It will be too late then."

"My head feels awful," I said. "You gave me so much brandy. It was good, good to make us talk then, but now we need a break. Sleep."

"It was you who wanted to wait for breakfast," he reminded me.

I wanted to reply, yes, but that was before your voice turned nasty, before you began to show the bad side effects of drink.

"Anyway, all I wanted to tell you was I think you were an awful father. You hated children. You wanted them, but you hated them for being children. Francis and I lived divorced from you. You just hid yourself away writing until we grew into an age that was interesting to you."

"Stop," I said.

"Too painful?" he asked viciously.

"Yes, if you must know," I replied. "Now I want to go to my room. Perhaps we should stay another day. I am free to stay another day."

"I'm not," he said. "I have business to finish in Barcelona."

"With Luis?"

"With myself."

"Then you are not going to come back with me to England?" I asked.

"No. There are reasons why I have to go back to Spain."

"Emotional reasons?" I replied. "It can't be to do with money. You are not in need of money."

"Call it what you like," he said.

As he finished the sentence I felt the room around me begin to reel, as if I was on a rough sea. I hurriedly asked him to remind me where the nearest toilet was. He pointed to a door behind where we were sitting, and I just about made it there in time. I vomited, half into the toilet, half onto the floor. This had the almost instantaneous effect of making me cold and totally sober at the same time. I hugged myself roughly with my arms, and then started to stamp my feet on the floor. I thought absurdly this would somehow make me warm. He can't leave me today, I said to myself as I continued stamping my feet. Like a child who cannot get his own way. He cannot abandon me. We must go back to England together. He is all I have left, and he cannot leave me now. There was no sanity left in the emotional desolation I felt, but eventually I calmed down, throwing water onto my face and then drinking water from the tap.

I went back into the foyer. He was asleep on the sofa, and there was still no one at the reception desk. I looked around at the hotel, knowing I would remember it always. At that moment in time it was all of Paris to me. The Paris that had lost me one son and had made me aware of my second. I looked down at him, blessedly alone with him. I took in the way he was curled up on the sofa, the way his head rested on his arm as a pillow. I saw his dark hair fall over his eyes, and then noticed his body was twitching in his sleep. I wondered what he was dreaming, and intruder that I was, I wanted to enter somehow into him and share in his dreams. He looked so handsome. I fought the desire to bend down and kiss him. I knew if I did, I would want him to take me in his arms and hold me close. I stared like this for a long time, not moving once in case he woke, and all the time I thanked whatever fate it was that had left us alone together in such a public place. Then I watched as slowly he woke up. He looked up at me watching him and then with boyish awkwardness got to his feet. He swayed slightly as he stood there.

"I must go to bed," he said.

"Yes," I replied.

"Three hours sleep only," he said, "and then I'll wake you. We have to find the times of trains and buy tickets."

I nodded my head in silence.

"We won't even leave from the same station," I murmured.

"I know," he replied. "I hate goodbyes at stations."

Part Three
The Return

The Eurostar arrived on time at St Pancras. I felt totally exhausted, and when I changed trains it was in a sort of stupor. It was very late when I opened the door of the house, and as soon as I entered I realised that now it was going to be unendurable to be alone. Dreading sleep and possible nightmares, I took the bedding off my bed and laid it on the living room floor. Without taking off my clothes I threw myself down on it and fell asleep almost at once. Mercifully there were no dreams, good or bad, and I awoke to the sound of letters falling on the mat in the hallway. When I went to get them there was nothing personal there, only a handful of bills, but who was left who would want to contact me? I could only think, this was how it was going to be for the rest of my life. When they were in the house I wanted to be alone, and now . they were out of the house I could not bear the thought. Those who wish for solitude when others are around find, when they get their wish, that it is hell. And the house was so quiet. It added stillness upon imposed stillness with a heavy, dull weight. To do something, anything, I cleaned the place, room after room. I did not notice objects, but just cleaned them. I had to make myself active, physically active. Above all I could not face sitting in my study and contemplating any work. My study was the one room I could not go into, that I could not clear out. Once in there, I told myself, it will be a prison.

After the housework I went for a long walk. I looked at other houses, going up to windows and peering into them. After the pounding rhythms of Paris the place seemed so remote and lifeless. Even the rooms I looked into had no one in them to stare back, to shout at me to go away. It was as if everyone had died. Even the park in the late afternoon, the park where I had tried to keep Francis from leaving, was quiet. I stood by the lake and there were no small ships, either sailing out into the water or making their way back. There were no children at all in the park, only a few people walking quickly through, as if showing by their purposeful step that this was the last place they wanted to be. The park was a shortcut for them, not a destination. I looked up at the sky and saw how grey it was, how there was no hope of an evening sun. Even the air was cold, but I was so wrapped up in my solitude I failed to feel it. I began to feel disorientated, so I lowered my head and zigzagged my way back to the house. I was in no way drunk, but my legs would not allow me to walk in a straight line. It would have been too simple, and the prospect of my future in this place was simplicity itself: a simplicity . I could not even begin to contemplate with rational thought.

Autumn brought days when the sky was the colour of grey flesh, and towards the horizon, wound gashes of red spilled out horizontally and then fell downwards. The autumn days were constant in their dullness, in their smell of decay. Then winter came with its first snows, and I shut myself within the house, silence my only companion, and an aching need for sexuality that could not be relieved. I masturbated daily, and in my bedroom, as I wiped away the drying sperm, an inner voice repeated, *Man is suspended between God and youth.* As I heard these words repeat themselves in my brain, I knew I did not understand them. I neither understood what God meant for me anymore nor what youth meant for me anymore. The only form of youth I possessed in my mind was the form of my son Francis. He was, with his fair hair, a god to me, but he was not God. I had no relationship with God that was possible. As for the young, the body of my lost son was the only sexual stimulus I allowed to bring me to orgasm. But still the words repeated themselves: *Man is suspended between God and youth,* and I knew I had read them somewhere. Somewhere long ago I had read these words, and now in my seemingly endless solitude they were the only response my mind could offer to this solitude. After all, I had chosen this solitude. I had disconnected phones, and I now avoided the letters that piled up on the floor. I deliberately chose to have no more contact with the outside world. If I was to be alone, then I must be completely alone. Of this I was sure, and yet in this very core of being sure, I fought off the marginal terror that God could perhaps exist, that he could be there within or without, and that he was relentlessly spying on me. As the winter advanced it grew to be an obsession. What if this God, that I felt had departed or ceased to exist, was there after all, hidden like a spider or a rat in the corner of my rooms, staring out as I pulled upon my penis, as I cried out Francis's name? When I was not conjuring up sexual images of my son I tried to read, but my mind would not focus. Sometimes I would try to listen to music on the radio, but all sounds began to sound sinister. Contemporary music especially, sounded violent and full of aggression. I felt if I let these sounds really enter my mind, I would go completely mad. I began to be afraid of everything, and could only get a few hours' sleep if I kept the light on. I bathed less frequently, and after a while I was conscious that both my body and my clothes smelt. When I took off my clothes I was afraid my flesh had rotted. I never took off my clothes to masturbate and often climaxed over my shirt and trousers. As I seldom changed, the pervasive odours of urine and sperm became a part of me. I also shaved less, and my face looked older because of it. Sometimes I thought I heard noises in the corners of the rooms, sudden inexplicable sounds of movement, and in my mind I said: this is the terror of it. The terror of God's presence is here: a dark, merciless God watching every gesture, every futile attempt at pleasuring my body. I cried in an attempt to release emotion, but my tears were a sham and inside I was dry. One night, unable to endure the possibility of an unseen presence, I cried out, "Show yourself. You have me. So show yourself. You see me in my every action. You judge or you don't judge. I know you watch my hand jerking at my penis. I know you see the images in my mind. I know you see how I spread the arse of my son wide open. I know you see me ejaculate over his blond hair and onto his face. I know you are a witness, because it is true that I am suspended between you and his young flesh."

Then for a while there would be no sounds at all. Total silence would return. Silence broken only by the winter wind, or the lashing of rain at the windows. The anguish of my condition became most acute during a storm. My head would do strange things, and in my eyes I would see colours that appeared to come from within myself. Vivid slashing greens and orange, brilliant and overwhelming. They, more than anything, made me aware I was slipping further and further into madness. It was only when the storms stopped that I saw clearly again, and I began to dread the change of the elements outside. I wanted, had to have, utter silence and utter stillness. Even as I came over my hand I did not cry out. I did not even dare break the necessary silence by saying aloud Francis's name.

It was like this until the beginning of March. I endured the hell I was in all through the autumn and most of the winter. But during the early days of March, I felt a kind of sanity return. I masturbated less. I washed more and even washed my clothes. I didn't know why this change was occurring, but it was. I began to breathe more easily and slept for longer hours at night.

"I don't want to need images of my son. I don't want to use images of his body in my mind. I cannot soil him or myself any longer."

I said this aloud to myself daily, and daily it gave me more strength. It was like a mantra that by repetition brought me more light, more security and less fear. I read tentatively again, and then found I could read a book in a few days, able at last to retain some of what I had just read. In this way, during the month of March, I stabilised myself. I even felt a need to open the pile of letters, to make myself available by phone, but as soon as I moved to do both, I drew back. I realised I could only remain in this precarious state of stability if I kept the outside world truly out. During the months of self-incarceration I only went out once a week to get a minimum of food in. I kept myself alive on cereal and biscuits and bowls of soup. My mirror told me how thin I had become.

March left with a thunderous storm, but my vision was not affected by it. I just sat in a chair, closed my eyes and pressed my hands over my ears until it passed. The following day, the first of April, I opened the front door of the house early and went for a walk just for the sake of it. I walked to the park. The weather was still cold, but I felt the onset of spring. As I was about to leave the park I saw him sitting on a bench, staring vacantly into space. It was Thomas. I felt a tightening in my throat. How long had he been back? When had he come back? Why hadn't he come to me? The questions beat against my brain. I also had a desire to run from him, to turn away from him. As far as I could tell he was unaware of my presence, and I could go back to the house and leave him there.

Thomas.

I said his name to myself, realising that for months I had not thought of him. My sole obsession had been with sexual thoughts of Francis, and in that obsession there had been no room for memories of Paris or what I had felt for Thomas there. I realised with total clarity that Paris had brought him to me, while returning to this so-called home in England had only managed to drive his image away. I could not explain it, but it was true. I had been mad, and in that madness there had been no room for Thomas.

Tentatively, I decided to move forward. I walked very, very slowly to the bench. I put my hand out and from behind him put my shaking fingers onto his shoulder. He started and turned. He looked older, much older than I remembered him in Paris. I wondered if he too had gone through a period of intense madness.

"You," I said simply.

"Yes," he replied, and his face was creased by a forced smile.

"Why here? In this park? Why didn't you come home?"

The word home was difficult to say. Did I still consider the house to be his home? As I questioned within, I knew that I did.

"Last night I came to the house," he said. "I was outside banging on the door for a long time. The light was on. You were in."

"I only heard the storm," I said.

"But I knocked again and again."

His voice was harsh and reproachful.

"I covered my ears during the storm. I couldn't bear the sound. That's why I didn't hear you."

He laughed at this and turned his head away. I could see he was disbelieving.

"So what did you do?" I asked.

"Walked."

"In the storm? All night?"

"The hotel was closed. There was nowhere for me to go. And there has been no way to contact you for months. You have no idea how many times I tried."

"No," I said. "I have no idea."

"You cut off all means of contact. I had to remain in Barcelona, and I hated worrying something had happened to you. It wasn't fair."

The last words were said like a hurt child. The tone in his voice was bruised, and I felt ashamed of my madness that had so brutally separated me from him.

"I was sick," I said.

"How sick?"

"In my mind. I was sick in my mind. I am sorry, but there

was nothing I could do about it except attempt to defeat it, which I hope I have."

"I don't understand," he replied.

"I don't expect you to. But come home now."

He got up from the bench and looked at me warily. I saw the question in his eyes: does he really mean this? I touched him on the arm. It felt good to touch him, but I felt him shrink slightly from my touch.

"Let's go," he said.

We walked back to the house in silence, and once inside he said nothing. He went straight to his room and to bed. I heard him get up once during the remainder of the day to go to the toilet, but I did not see him until the following morning. He came downstairs, said a sullen hello and slumped into a chair.

"I haven't much food in the house," I said.

He turned and looked at me. His face seemed to twitch with suppressed anger.

"What were you doing?" he said. "Starving yourself to death?"

I did not reply, but added I could make him coffee.

"I can go out and get food if I'm hungry, and no thank you, I don't want coffee. Or tea."

"You are still angry with me, aren't you?"

I stood in front of him. Intimidated by my nearness, he got up and moved over to a window. He looked outside.

"What sort of a sickness in the head was it, Francis?"

He used my name. He did not call me Father. He used my name. I felt a rush of warmth inside me at the sound of my name on his lips.

"It was terrible," I said simply.

"That's not explaining it."

"I can't do that. Not yet."

He turned and faced me.

"Did you really have to cut off all methods of communication? And my letters? Didn't you open one of them?"

I shook my head as if disbelieving myself.

"How many did you write?" I asked.

"You must have received them. You should know."

"I haven't opened any letters for months," I said slowly. "See for yourself. They are all piled up over there."

I pointed to a sideboard. He went over. Going through them one by one, he set three official-looking letters aside.

"There are bills that are not even paid," he said. "You're lucky you have electricity."

"Yes," I replied.

"I'll pay it today," he said. I don't want the electricity to stop, even if you don't mind.

"I'm sorry," I murmured. My voice sounded weak and foolish. This must have been the clinching factor, for he suddenly threw all the letters on the floor and hit the sideboard violently with his hands.

"Damn you!" he cried.

"Do you think it was my fault?" I shouted back.

"Yes," he said. "I do. I was there, and you didn't leave one way open for me. I thought we had got close in Paris, but now I see it was all a fraud. All a great big nothing."

He made a big, wide, circular gesture with his hand.

"I said I didn't expect understanding," I replied more calmly, "and I don't. I was mad. I can't explain madness."

"Yes, you were," he said, and his voice was now nearly as calm as mine. He went back to the chair and sat in it again, staring at me with a hard, questioning look.

"Do you want me to go?" he asked suddenly. "My bags are still at the station. I put them in a locker when I knew I wasn't going to get into either the hotel or this house."

"No, I don't want you to go. I want you to stay."

He smiled then and shrugged.

"It's my brother, isn't it?" he said. "He drove you to whatever it was you went through."

"I don't know," I replied. My face felt flushed. I thought of all the sexual positions I had put Francis in, in my mind. I did not feel ashamed of the fact, only numbed by the absurdity of my obsession.

"Well, he has gone for good," he said at last.

"You have heard from him?"

"Twice. On the phone. He rings me occasionally. He changes his mobiles all the time so as not to be found." He paused, and then added, "Wouldn't you call that a sort of madness as well? He has shut himself off, just like you."

"So you have no idea where he is?"

There was a slight tremor in my voice as I asked this.

"I have an idea he may be in Africa. I think he mentioned Africa in one of his calls. It sort of slipped out. But I have no idea where."

"Is he still with –?" I left her name unsaid.

"Yes."

My stomach heaved with a violent motion of sickness. I put my hand over my mouth, and in this action somehow prevented myself from vomiting. I saw Francis in the arms of the woman, and she was touching him in different ways from how I had imagined touching him. I couldn't imagine her opening his buttocks and putting her tongue to his anus.

"I hate her," I said slowly.

He did not respond to this. He only mumbled that he would get some food in, and without another word went out of the house. For a moment I thought he was leaving for good, and I did not want him to go. I cried out, but he had already gone. It was then that the sickness returned, and I went to the bathroom. Later, after I had retched up everything that was inside me, I returned to the living room and then went into the kitchen. I made myself a strong cup of coffee and sat at the table. I was sitting there when Thomas returned with a bag full of shopping.

"I'll make breakfast," he said, and promptly went about making it in silence. He boiled eggs and cut thick slices of bread. He toasted them, and put marmalade on the table. We did not speak during this whole procedure, and when he put a boiled egg in front of me I forced myself to eat it. I refused the rest.

"You look terrible," he said.

I laughed then to break the tension.

"So do you," I replied. "On top of that you look old. Older than me."

"It's not surprising," he said with a joking reproachfulness. "Walking as I did last night. Seeing this town. It was as if I had never seen it before, all closed in, locked up, refusing entrance. You know, I could have knocked on any door, and they would not have taken me in."

"You don't know that," I said.

"The curtains all tightly drawn. The gardens, neat and cold, and the rain coming down. The wind making strange noises in the trees. And yet –" he paused.

"Yet what?"

"I still found it interesting. The sameness of it. The neat Victorian houses and the Edwardian terraces, once such simple places, turned into houses for our new up and coming generation. All simplicity gone. But I expect it was smug even back then. Not like Paris."

"Paris is smug too," I said.

He bit into a large slice of toast, and marmalade dribbled down his chin. I recalled a scene from many years ago when I had seen him in a similar state, sitting at the table covered in raspberry jam. I laughed at the thought.

"What?" he said with his mouth full. "Am I so funny?"

"The raspberry jam," I replied. "You were about three years old, and all alone in this kitchen. You had smeared too much jam on your bread, and most of it rubbed off onto your face. You had a large slice of bread like you have now, and you were cramming too much of it into your mouth –"

"Just like now," he interrupted.

"Perhaps worse then," I said. "Your whole face was raspberry red, and you just wiped it with the back of your hand and then licked most of it into your mouth."

"You saw that?"

He said this, and there was a note of wonder in his voice.

"You can remember that?"

"Yes," I replied.

"But how can you? You never came into the kitchen to have breakfast with either of us boys. You never bothered with us."

"But I did see you. I can remember it clearly. Maybe I was looking into the kitchen on the way back to my study."

"Yes, it must have been that," he said, and crunched on the toast.

"Was Francis with me?" he asked, his mouth full again. He looked like the child he had once been.

"I can't remember him," I said.

He got up then and cleared away the plates and the cups. He stood at the sink and did the washing up, very slowly and very carefully, not missing one thing that needed to be washed. I noticed how every detail seemed to count. He looked like a young boy trying to be an adult standing there. I asked if I could help, and he said no, he was perfectly capable of taking on these jobs now we were alone together in the house.

"Do you mind us being alone here?" I asked. "I mean, I'm not famous for keeping you company, am I?"

"I didn't have much company in Barcelona, so why should I need it now? Anyway, I can feel your presence nearby. That's enough."

"Did you do this for Luis?"

I don't know why I asked. A perversity of sorts. I told myself the question wasn't meant to cause emotional harm, or regret.

"Luis died," he said, and began to put the cutlery away.

"What do you mean, died?"

"He had cancer."

I thought of Aids at once, and as if reading my thoughts he said, "No, it wasn't Aids-related. He had a tumour on the brain. I knew it when we first met, but I didn't allow it to get in the way of the relationship we had."

"Is that why you never fell in love with him?" I asked.

"No," he said simply, drying his hands with a towel. He then returned to the table and sat facing me. "Luis never turned what was happening to him into emotional blackmail."

He paused and looked down at the table, as if inspecting the grains in the wood.

"You don't have to continue," I said.

"That was the unfinished business I had to go back to. That was what I had to stay in Barcelona for. We had stopped being lovers, but I still had to be his friend. His family were out of their minds with distress, but I managed to keep sane. And then when the end came it was relatively sudden, and considering the nature of cancer, he died a dignified death."

He laughed, and then added how he hated the dignity of death, but how it had made it so much better for Luis.

"It is not dignified for a boy not much older than me to die like that. You sit by the bed and you know God has turned his face away."

"I should have read your letters. I should have answered them," I said.

"But I didn't write about him in the letters. I couldn't write about it. I don't even know how I am capable of talking about it now. His death made me hate that fucking trendy city."

"Well, it isn't trendy back here," I said, and then felt afraid I had been too flippant. "No wonder you look older," I added.

Older, I thought, but still a child in some ways. Then the shame of my own closing off, of my own shutting down, hit me. I felt mad at myself for being mad, for letting obsession rule me, and giving in to the desolation of a lost desire. And the thought came to me that it would come again, that in all possibility the insane feelings would return and once again I would be helpless in front of them. I had not finished with my struggle, or with my battle with the fair angel who was my departed son. Even now I was pretending to be alright. If I dared to look closer, I would still see the shadows lurking within, once more ready to make their appearance and unbalance me. As if to torture me further with this premonition of what may return, I saw a picture in my mind of a naked Francis, lying on a bed with his legs wide apart, masturbating in front of me. I cried out at the thought, cried out in a way I had never done when I had been alone with my fantasies.

"What is it?" Thomas asked.

"I was thinking of what you must have suffered," I lied.

He stared at me and smiled in a way I thought of as shyly, and said he was reconciling himself to it.

The rest of the day passed in outside activity. We went for a long walk together, out of the town and into the neighbouring countryside. The air was still wintry, but spring was there, waiting as it were in the wings to reveal itself. At a roadside café we stopped and had a meal. He ate heartily, and once more I recalled the child I had briefly seen eating a large chunk of toast. It was a persistent image from that time onwards, and still is. As the day slid towards evening we walked slowly back and quietly read, side by side, on the sofa in the living room.

This quiet, this peace, lasted until I began to hear noises again. In my bedroom I heard voices coming from the corners of the room. To banish them I had a light on every night, but slowly I realised the obsession over Francis was returning. This time it was taking a new form. I imagined he was hiding in the house, hiding from both of us, and that he had returned. I thought at first he had died far away in Africa, or wherever he had been, and that his ghost had returned. This was the first step in the spiral downwards of my delusions.

The turning point occurred one night when I was alone in my room. I started to sob uncontrollably. I tried everything to stop. I forced my fist into my mouth, and then when that failed clenched my teeth so tightly that the anguished sound could only be heard as a long, thin wailing at the back of my throat. Tears poured down my face, and there was nothing in me but this overwhelming need to let go. At last, unable to prevent the sound from travelling, I lay back on the bed and howled. I howled like an animal, and was past caring who heard. The next thing I felt was my body being shaken by strong hands, and between my cries and my sobs I heard Thomas screaming at me to stop.

"What is it? What is it?"

His pleas for me to stop mingled with questioning, "Are you in pain? Should I get in a doctor?"

I cried, and then I laughed. I could not speak, but the wailing continued, and in a blur I saw his concerned face approaching mine.

"You are killing yourself," he said. "You are killing yourself."

He shook me harder, lifting me off the bed. I stood in front of him, held up by him, my body held up like a puppet.

"Let me die," I at last said, the words strangled: a panting, almost incomprehensible exclamation of despair.

"I love you," he murmured. "I cannot let you die."

The words cut into my brain like a surgeon's knife. I felt a sudden lifting of a weight, and the next moment his lips were on mine. He was kissing me on the mouth.

At first I gave in to the kiss, wanting it, opening my mouth in response. His tongue lapped at the mixture of tears and saliva, and his body tightened harder against mine. Then I began to struggle, and with a violent push I pushed him from me.

"Not you," I shouted.

I had found my voice. It was as loud as my sobbing had been. I stood there, unsteadily, the room rocking. I looked at him. He was shaking with the shock of what he had just done. My mind was clear. My vision was clear. I felt my wet face drying, and brushed my lips where he had kissed me with the back of my hand.

"Not you," I repeated.

"Who then?" he said.

"No one. No one."

"That's not true," he replied.

I saw his face, white against the dark of his eyes and hair. He glowed with a terrible whiteness in the darkness of the room.

"No one has –"

"Kissed you?" he shouted back.

I wiped my mouth again with my hand, and as I did this he hit out at me, hitting my hand away with his own.

"It's not true," he said. "What of Francis? He would not be no one, would he? What if he had kissed you?"

"No one," I repeated mechanically. Then I added, wrenching the words from myself, "Francis is dead."

He stared at me without replying, then shook his head from side to side.

"It is not true," he said. "It's all in your mind."

"He died in a faraway place, but I know his presence is here. He has returned to us. He is in this house."

He came towards me then, and holding me in his arms caressed the back of my head.

"Don't," I said, but I lay against him, and I rested my head on his shoulder, crying silently.

"You must not think these thoughts," he said gently. His fingers descended from the back of my head to my neck. He pressed there tightly with them, massaging the pressure he imagined I had there. The warmth of his touch and the firmness of the massage made me ache inside for a closer union. I wanted him at that moment. I wanted his hands to reach down my back, to clasp me there and draw me inwards to his body. I felt with a sudden fear that he was aware of my sexual excitement.

"Don't," I repeated finally, and he let me go. I sat on the bed and hid my face in my hands.

"Francis is not here," he said. His voice was steady and sure. How could I not believe what he was saying? It sounded so right and so true. I was deluding myself. I was giving in to my imagination.

"Look at me," he ordered.

I took my hands away and looked at him. He remained at a distance, and I no longer saw Thomas my son, but a stranger. Even his features looked different. I thought, you are not made from my flesh. You are totally other. I have no relationship with you at all.

"No one," I repeated.

"What do you mean?" he asked.

"No one left. Francis gone. Thomas gone. No one."

"But I am here. I am Thomas, and I love you. Don't you know that?"

"No, I don't know that. I don't even know who you are."

He knelt before me. He took my hands into his hands. He rubbed my hands. He stared into my face, and as he did so the stranger's face I had imposed upon him melted. It was as if dead flesh was literally falling away from him, and there beneath I saw again the features of my young son.

"You cannot save me from myself," I said. "And you cannot save me from believing the spirit of Francis is in this house."

"What have you heard," he said gently. He was father now to me and being quietly patient as he asked me questions.

"Tell me what you have heard. Or have you seen something?"

"Not yet," I replied simply. "But I will see him, Thomas. I will see evidence soon of him being here."

"You are hoping he will be here in some form. Living or dead. Don't you see that's all it is?"

I looked around me then, staring into the corners of the room. The corners of the room were mocking me, and it was in them, in their darkness, that an invisible power would eventually drive me mad.

"I can only see in the centre of things," I said. "I cannot see in the corners. It is from there he will emerge. Eventually.

When it is time."

"Your brain is overwrought. You spent too much time alone here without anybody. There was no one here for you." He paused. "And then I show my love for you in the way that I did –"

This sentence jolted me back into some sort of other reality. Thomas, my son, had kissed me. He had entered my mouth with his tongue. He had tasted my saliva. He had taken part of me into his own self.

"Is it true that you love me?" I said.

I felt quiet now inside. A hush had fallen between us. A quiet where everything that existed between us could at last be revealed.

"Yes."

He looked away, and I felt how vulnerable he was in this admission.

"How do you love me?" I persisted.

"I think you know," he said.

He knelt back on his haunches and then stared at me. His eyes looked feverish. I saw a look of panic.

"Maybe I should not know," I replied.

"The truth is the truth," he said.

"Not always, Thomas."

"But in this case it is true. I told you about Luis. I told you I couldn't love him in the way he wanted me to, and I also said there was a reason for it that I was not ready to tell."

He drew in his breath sharply, and then whispered, "You were the reason. I am in love with you. I began desiring you in my early adolescence. I would catch glimpses of you. You never came to us, and I longed for you to come to us. Then before I went to Barcelona when we talked, I fought against the inner feelings I was hiding even from myself. Once in Barcelona I realised that only an older man could satisfy me sexually and that you, you my father, were that ideal of an older man."

I could not reply. I saw his eyes shine, and I knew this was a truth for him. Only a short while before when he had seemed other, he was other. He was the form of the lover. The lover who had taken the place of my son. I had seen it, and then it had melted away. But having caught sight of the lover I could not deny it was the innermost part of my child.

"I know you cannot say anything," he said.

He stood up, walked away and stood by the door.

"When I heard you howling in here, like a wounded animal, I too thought I would become crazy. I wanted to give my life for you if it could restore you to yourself, if it would take you away from the memory of my brother."

He looked at me for a brief moment, then opening the door went out. I heard him run along the landing, down the stairs and slam the front door. He had gone out into the night.

Days and nights I waited until he returned, and when he did return he did not return alone.

During those days and nights I remained in the house. I had enough food and drink not to have to go into town. I ate very little and drank lots of water. Sometimes I listened to music on the radio. I listened a lot to Radio 3. At one point I heard Callas singing *Madama Butterfly*, the end of act one. I had heard and seen the opera in my youth and disliked it. I disliked all Puccini. The nauseating sentimentality of the music made me think of arms wanting me, destroying me. I imagined the obscenity of words of romantic love, of tears shed because of that so-called love. I listened to the tenor calling her. Come, come, he was saying, and in it I heard the sadism that is at the heart of all this kind of sentimentality. The flaccid softness of the need to be plundered, to be grasped and used in one's body, and to sing one's response with rapture in return. I felt again the pressure of Thomas's lips on mine, and the mingling wetness of our mouths. The fluid of this emotional embrace I heard in the music, clinging, insatiable and poisoned by the flow of sexual desire: his and mine. But when I turned the radio off, killing the music just as it was drawing to its end, I knew whatever existed or would exist between Thomas and myself was made of something harder. The sadism of romance I had heard in Puccini was very different from the prospect of finding myself as a lover in Thomas's arms. I could not imagine how it would be, what sort of feelings I would have, or what sort of name I would give it. Instead of thinking of him, my thoughts returned to the body of Francis. In my imagination there was a closed room. In it, Francis and I could do battle with love for as long as we wanted, for as long as the masturbation ritual took for me to come. I would never have Francis in reality, but the reality of Thomas was an actual possibility. If of course he returned to the house. There were times during those days of his absence when I hoped he would never return, but then as contradiction is the name of the beast that is man I would hope the opposite. I wanted the door to open. I wanted to see him in the flesh.

He returned in the middle of the night. I was in bed. I heard him open the front door, and very loudly I heard his voice in the hall. I thought for a moment he was calling for me, and then quickly noticed he was speaking to someone else. He had brought someone back with him to the house. I heard another man's voice reply: a deep voice asking if it was alright to go upstairs to Thomas's room. I could tell by the tone of the voice and the sound in Thomas's reply that they were both drunk. I heard swearing from the other man as he climbed the stairs. He said "shit" as he tripped and then, "this is fucking madness." To Thomas's loud question asking if he was alright the man replied, "Of course I'm fucking alright." Did the man not know I was in the house? I assumed Thomas was perfectly aware of what he was doing despite his drunken tone of voice. He knew he was doing something he had never done before, and that I would dislike it in the house we shared.

The door of his room closed with a bang. After a short while I left my room and went along the landing. I stood there in the darkness and heard them clink glasses. Thomas said how glad he was they had managed to find the whisky. Then there was silence and a heavy fall. I heard the bed respond to the fall, and quietly at first, then growing in strength, I heard the sounds of physical contact. Groans, then cries of "fuck, fuck," and a shrill screaming sound. I could not make out if it was Thomas or the man screaming with pleasure, and I felt sick in my stomach. I saw a light coming out from the keyhole. In the darkness it beckoned to me to take on the posture of the ultimate humiliation: to kneel on the landing floor and put my eye to the keyhole to see what I could. The overhead light in Thomas's room was on, and I had a glimpse, only a glimpse, of the bed. I could not see the lower half of their bodies, but saw them naked from the chest upwards. Thomas was on top of the man, presumably penetrating him for the screaming squeals were coming from the man's prostrate body. Thomas heaved up and down on top of him, and between screams both he and Thomas would cry out the words "fuck, fuck." I saw the grimace of lust on Thomas's face. The rictus of desire was reaching its climax, the features distorting and the face, in its features, splitting apart. I could not see the man's face as Thomas came, but a few moments after, I saw Thomas move away out of sight. Then the man turned his head and faced the door as if he was looking directly at me. He was in his late forties or early fifties, and he had an ugly scar down the side of his bloated face. He was an ugly man. His mouth was open and a large protruding tongue was hanging out. I saw myself in the man and felt horror. I got up from my kneeling position and returned as quickly as I could back to my room. About an hour later I heard Thomas's door open. They did not talk to each other, or if they did it was in whispers, as I heard them go back down the stairs. The front door slammed shut. Expecting Thomas to return, I listened out for his steps, and then realised that he had left the house with the man.

The following morning he was back. I was sitting in the kitchen when he returned. He had a bag full of groceries and put them on the table.

"You haven't been out, have you?" he asked flatly.

I didn't reply to him. I didn't want to look at him.

"I said –"

"I know what you said. I heard you."

He sat down in front of me at the table and began to unpack tea and bread and the rest of the stuff until I told him to stop.

"I heard you," I repeated.

His face was drawn and tired, and he looked at me wearily across the table. He suddenly looked young and ridiculous, holding a pack of *Coco Pops* in his hand. He stopped unpacking as I had asked him to and put down the cereal along with the rest of the things.

"Can I make some coffee?" he asked as if he was a visitor and didn't live in the place after all.

"Go ahead."

He made the coffee. The room smelt alive with the aroma of it, and it smelt like the mockery of an ideal home. The smell you create to make people welcome. He sat down again and sipped at his coffee nervously. Obviously he was hung over from the drink, and was trying hard not to show it.

"Bad head?" I asked.

He nodded, and put the cup down on the table. I could not recognise this boy in front of me as being the person who had brought the older man, as old as me, back the night before, but I wasn't yet ready to challenge him with that.

"How long have you been drinking?" I asked.

"I've drunk a bit for years," he said. "Francis did too. There were many times when he and I sneaked in a bottle and drank it secretly in one of our bedrooms. After we'd finished it, one of us was responsible for getting rid of the bottle."

"That's kids' play," I said. "I did that too when I was

young. I was eleven when I had my first secret bottle."

He looked at me and smiled. He thought I was suddenly being friendly, and his face relaxed a little. He finished off his coffee and went to pour himself another cup.

"That's not what I meant though," I added. "When did you start becoming a drunk?"

Sensing the hostility in my voice, he stiffened and came back to the table slowly and carefully as if avoiding glass on the floor.

"I'm not a drunk," he said.

"No?" I queried. "What about –"

I stopped, then showing my own sense of frustration hurled the groceries he had brought off the table. They fell, and a carton of milk split open. It covered the floor with a gush of white liquid. He was about to pick the things up when once again I told him to stop.

"Leave them," I said.

He drew himself up and stared at me hard.

"What is it you want to say?" he asked.

"About last night."

"Oh."

"What do you mean, oh?"

"Is that what you meant about hearing?" he asked.

Now I was really angry. I felt so angry I wanted to hit him. I laughed at the thought that I had never hit either of my children, but now I very much needed to punch him in the face.

"Yes," I said and clenched my hands under the table. I clenched them so tightly I felt pain. It was good to feel the pain.

"Was he the fuck you wanted?" I asked.

He got up from the table then and made as if to leave the room. I jumped up and managed to get to the door before him. I pushed him back into the room, pushed him so hard that he nearly fell.

"I was drunk," he mumbled.

"Lover! What a lover you were!"

"I was drunk," he shouted. "I can hardly remember bringing him back here at all."

"But you do remember, don't you?"

"Yes."

"And you haven't answered my question. Was he a good fuck?"

"That's not what happened," he said.

"I heard it all. The screaming pig sound. All of it."

I was about to say I had degraded myself by going onto my knees and had peered through the keyhole of his room, but I couldn't go that far.

"We had nowhere else to go. He is married, and there was no question of going to his place."

"Couldn't you have done it up against some wall in a back alley?" I jeered at him.

"No."

"Why? Animals do it. You sounded like animals. It was a fine imitation of a rut to my ears."

He shook his head and backed away from me, backed into one of the corners of the room.

"Having fun humiliating me?" he asked.

"Not particularly," I said, "but did you have fun making so much noise, so much noise it was obvious I would hear it?"

"I was too drunk –"

He couldn't finish. He was silently crying, wiping away the tears with the back of his hands like a frightened child who has been dragged before a headmaster. I had looked like that once at school when I had been caught stealing from someone's locker. I knew the look well, and the childish rush of tears.

"Was he the best you could bring back?"

I told him the truth then.

"I saw his face. I looked through the keyhole in your door."

He dropped his hands to his sides. He shuddered, and still

the silent tears fell. I was as revolted by them as if I was having Puccini inflicted on me again.

"You disgust me," I said.

"So did the man," he answered. "So have all the older men I have been with. Here and in Barcelona. But I do it because I have to do it. I do it so as to drag myself through the mud. I do it to blot out your image, or worse, to remember it."

"Shut up," I shouted.

"Why?"

It was his turn now. The crying boy metamorphosed into an angry man. He spat out the next words as if some demon had suddenly possessed him, as if by being out of control he was very much in control.

"Tell me, Francis," he said.

"Tell you what?"

"Tell me how much the sounds we made turned you on. Did you have your own cock out while you were kneeling in front of my door? Did you?"

His eyes were black and hard. All trace of tears gone. Systematically, he smashed plates, cups, anything in the kitchen he could lay his hands on. He was in a fury, and I watched him in silence until he had finished wrecking half of the kitchen. When the attack was over he collapsed at the kitchen table and stared into space.

"I felt nothing but horror," I said quietly. "Horror at seeing the face of a man – yes, I did see his face – the face of a man who has just given himself to someone like you." I paused, and then added, "Maybe you have given him something. How do you know you haven't got some venereal disease after going with all these older men? Have you been tested? Have you thought of that? What if he infects his wife? Being married he might be too stupid to make sure he is in the clear himself?"

"I am not diseased," Thomas said coldly.

He picked up a knife lying on the table and began to play with it.

"Do you hear," he repeated. "I have no venereal disease."

He got up then and came towards me. He came close to my body and raised the knife to my throat.

"Put it down," I said.

"If I go with pigs, then I can cut pigs too," he answered.

"Don't be such a childish, bloody fool. Put that thing down, and then get out of this room."

His face was close to mine. So close he could have kissed me. Somewhere deep within me I wanted him to kiss me. The proximity of the knife was turning me on. Instead he smiled at me: a smile so enigmatic no words could describe it. It was filled with love, hatred and a multitude of impulses and emotions racing within him, and by the nearness of contact, racing within me. He then lifted the knife and with a threat that was more a gesture of tenderness, caressed my cheek with the blade. Then slowly, he lowered the knife, put it back on the table and left the room. I listened as he climbed the stairs and reaching his room gently opened the door, and equally gently closed it behind him. I picked up the knife from the table and unable to control myself, put out my tongue and licked at the handle he had grasped.

"Thomas."

That's all I said, then I began to clean up the kitchen. After a while I was overtaken by an attack of giddiness and just made it to my room. I think I passed out.

In a dream that seemed to be a waking hallucination I was on a train, conscious of trying to escape the country, to escape to Paris. I was going mad. I knew I was going mad, and I wanted to experience that madness to the full upon my return to Paris. The train hurtled through the night, and when I awoke it was still night. The train had stopped at a station. There was no one else in the carriage but me. I looked out of the window of the carriage. In the darkness I saw a brightly lit sign that said *Welcome to Brighton*. I got off the train confused and upset. I had to spend the night in a city that disturbed me. I wandered the streets, not wanting a hotel. I wanted to wait for the dawn, when I could get on a train to take me to London, and from there to Paris. I knew I had somehow made a mistake in accidentally coming here, an accident that had been totally out of my control and that I had no knowledge of. There was nothing to do except to wait for first light.

I wandered down to the sea. The waves pounded loudly on the shore, and a round grey-faced moon looked down. I heard a distant cacophony of sound and saw the Palace Pier lit up, all bright pink and blue. It was lurid against the dark rush of the waves, representing the worst this city by the sea had to offer. When I arrived at the entrance to the pier I saw a sign that said *House of Men* in harsh red lights. I thought of the brothel lights I had once seen in Amsterdam, and as I entered the red door that now was the only way onto the pier I saw the booths and game halls were all effectively brothels. Men stood outside, and other than them I was the only person along the whole length of the pier. The sounds I had heard from afar on my approach to this palace of pleasure were now almost deafening: old disco tunes and the voices of singers long since forgotten. A man outside one booth leered at me and knocked on the booth's curtained window. My son Francis appeared at the window, his face covered in make-up. He said words I could not hear, and the man said that for a price I could see Francis naked. I paid the price. The man knocked again at the window and the partially drawn curtains were then completely drawn back. Against a background of crazy mirrors that distorted everything in front of them, I saw my son, nude. His penis was erect and dripping sperm. He put out his tongue at me, then touched his penis and raised some of the white liquid to his lips. He gyrated, and his booth now stretched into a larger space: a space big enough to be a theatre. He danced and touched himself at the same time, and in the background the mirrors distorted his every movement. First he was a tall man, then a dwarf, then thin, then obscenely large. His red parted lips took up the space of the whole length of mirrors, opening wide as if ready to engulf me. Then in turn his penis magnified and shrank. I turned away, dizzy at the sight of him, and ran down the length of the pier, trying to avoid the pimps who were calling out to me. At the end, where the old ghost train used to be, I found an empty building. The ghosts had gone, and in their place was an apparently unused bar. I entered the place and, as I did so, heard Thomas's voice. I couldn't see him in the semi-darkness, but I heard his voice.

"This is all mine," he said. "It is my home. I own it all."

His voice rose over both the sound of the sea and the pounding retro music. I called to him; I called out his name.

"What more do you want?" he cried back. "Theatres and brothels are here. What more do you want?"

Then, very dimly, the lights in the bar came on. I saw him at the far end of the space, spot-lit on a makeshift stage. He was taking off his clothes slowly, invitingly, and his face was as impassive as a mask. I advanced towards him, and as I did so the mask-face cracked into life. He looked old. So old, I thought, he cannot be my son. This is my father or my grandfather, but not my son.

"Francis has to be paid to do it," he said, "but I do it for free. I am the gift. He is the bought object."

Then, brusquely interrupting, I heard the sound of angry voices in the background, a whole crowd of angry voices coming closer.

"We will get you," they cried. "We will destroy you and throw you into the sea. This will be your punishment for what you have done to our city."

Thomas laughed and continued to take off his clothes.

"We will die together," he cried out loudly. "You and I, Father will die together."

As he revealed his naked body to me the doors smashed open and a horde of old men entered the space, converging on us to take our lives. Thomas made obscene gestures at them and shouted words of abuse.

"Did they let you out of your retirement homes to come and destroy what you can no longer have? Why do you all pretend? You are jealous, not moral."

I awoke screaming at the moment they overpowered us. I awoke, or did I just imagine I had awoken? I got out of bed, opened the door of my room and by the feeble light of the landing I saw at my feet a white lily, and then another. A line of them led to the top of the stairs. On each step going down there was a lily, and in the hall below a mass of them piled up against the door. I felt I was suffocating. Instead of the floor I was treading on wet soil. Fighting my way through earth and flowers I flung the door open. Outside I drew in long, deep breaths, and as I reached the gate at the front of the garden a figure stepped out in front of me. I felt my body being shaken.

"What are you doing out here? You are naked."

I stared at Thomas who was staring down at my naked body. He pushed me back into the house. The hall was now empty. The flowers and the earth had gone.

"There was soil here and lilies," I said.

"You have been dreaming."

"A white line of lilies, leading from my room," I added. "It means there has been a death."

"Cover yourself," he said abruptly, and taking down an overcoat from a hall hanger, forced me to put it on.

"You were dreaming," he repeated, "walking in your sleep."

He pushed me into the living room. I felt ridiculous standing there, naked except for an overcoat, and miserably vulnerable.

"I don't sleepwalk," I replied.

"Obviously you do."

"I was dreaming before, but I woke up to find the flowers there. Also earth on the hallway floor."

"And where is the earth and where are the flowers now?"

His voice jeered at me, and I could see he was swaying slightly on his feet. He had been drinking again. I thought to myself, the boy is a hopeless drunk. I cannot deal with a drunk. But at the same time, there was a perverse desire in me to do combat, to touch him. It was as Edgar Allan Poe had called it, *The Imp of the Perverse*.

"You are drunk again," I said.

"So what if I am?"

"Someone put those flowers there," I insisted, "someone who knew I was alone. I believe it was meant to frighten me."

"Who?" he asked. "Who is this person then?"

"Francis," I said simply. I added to this by saying, "Francis has returned. He wants to frighten me. Catherine loved lilies. They were her favourite flowers. He is frightening me with memories of his mother. He hates me for her death."

The words poured out of me. I knew as I was saying them they had no substance in what is called reality, and yet at the same time I wondered, what if this is the reality? What if this is true? He has come back. He has taken earth from his mother's grave and brought it into the house.

"Francis," Thomas shouted. "I am tired of hearing the sound of his bloody name. You haunt me and yourself with his name. He has gone for good. Can't you get it into your head? He has left us, and he won't ever come back."

"Not true," I replied. "You don't know that."

"I do. Shut up about him. I hate him."

He came up to me and breathed alcoholic fumes into my face.

"You and your obsession with him," he cried.

Then he ripped at my overcoat, and in a moment he had taken it from my body. There I was, standing in the bright light of the room, naked in front of him. I remembered Francis dancing in the brothel on the pier. I remembered Thomas himself standing there in the bar revealing himself to me and to the crowd of angry men. In my shock I began to dance in front of Thomas in the living room.

"Don't do that," he screamed, and lunged at me. I avoided him and danced across the room to the door. It's easy, I thought absurdly, to dance away from a drunk. I was conscious of my exposed genitals bouncing up and down, and I wanted to mock him with them, as both he and his brother had mocked me on the pier. I was also saying, in this obscene and ridiculous gesture, I am unyielding and you can never have me. I am the older man you cannot possess. But as I got to the door, spinning in my dance, the room revolving around me, I felt blows on my body. Thomas was hitting me on the chest, in the face and on the thighs.

"I wish Francis was dead," he kept on saying. "I wish I could kill him now."

"So what do you want?" I screamed between the blows, smarting from his hard flesh on my flesh, feeling the savage pain. "What do you want to do? Kill me instead?"

Before he answered I escaped from him. I ran up the stairs to the landing and got into my room in time. Moments later he was pounding on the door, asking to be let in. His voice had changed. All brutality was gone. He was now begging, and there were sobs. He said he loved me and he only hated Francis because I loved him.

"Why can't I be as good as Francis for you?" he cried. "Isn't my body as beautiful as his?"

I leant against the door and looked down at my bruised flesh. I saw he had drawn blood and that the top of my thigh was scratched and bleeding.

"Go to hell with your love," I shouted through the door. Then I heard him run down the stairs.

I was ill for the next few days. I had nothing in my room to clean my body, and in the state I was in I was afraid to leave what I now considered to be my sanctuary. I was sure Thomas would make an attempt on my life, and with this fear I nursed myself out of the shock I had suffered. I wanted to remain alive. If Francis was back, I wanted to be well enough to face him. Then I remembered the lilies from my wife's grave, and how I had been convinced they were real. Perhaps he had returned to kill me with even more determination than Thomas. After all, if it was he who had left the flowers and soil in the house, it could only have been done out of hatred. Whereas if Thomas were to kill, it would be motivated by love. The passion of my sons made me shiver with cold, and then a sudden heat made my flesh drip with sweat. Gemini. It was as if they were twins of a terrifying desire.

Afraid of what was beyond the door I used a corner of the room to defecate and urinate in. The rest of the time I slept, feverishly dreaming dreams of both horror and sexuality. In those endless dreams I was always the pursued, and the pursuer alternated between my two sons. Then one night I felt better, and at last I was brave enough to face what was outside the room.

I opened the door and crept along the landing. The silence of the house closed around me. No one was there but me. I showered and then cleaned up the body waste in my room. After I had completed that, I put on clean clothes and ate for the first time in days. I was ravenous. My throat was also parched with thirst. I ate and ate, and then drank and drank. Now, I said to myself, you must go out. You must breathe fresh air.

I felt almost drunk as I gulped in the air and walked away from the house. I looked up at the cloudless night sky. I was moon-caught. It glowed at me, bigger than I could ever remember it having been. It seemed nearer to the earth than I had seen it before. I could see the dark lines of dead seas and mountain ranges criss-crossing the vivid landscape of white. I was caught in its spell of nightmare: the nightmare of all those who cannot rest when the moon is so near and so bright. I walked along the long road that led me to the churchyard just beyond the town. Instinctively, I made my way to my wife's grave, as if I already knew that I would be met there, either by the living or the dead, or both. When I reached the grave I saw fresh lilies had been placed upon it. I knelt facing the headstone, conscious of its dark form looming over me. Then as I looked up, the form moved, and I felt the sickness of fear again as Thomas moved towards me. Neither of us spoke. He knelt beside me, and then as if it was the most natural thing in the world he pushed me down upon the grave itself. Silently, and with a certain amount of gentleness, he pulled my trousers down. I closed my eyes, knowing what he would do. I heard him remove his own lower clothing, and then I felt him lower himself upon my body. He fondled my back and my buttocks for a long time, finger-penetrating me at first, and then with a sudden thrust he forced himself inside me. I cried out, I fought, but he was too strong for me and eventually my body relaxed.

At last I am in love.

Inside me the thought battled with the pain of penetration. My own hot, red blood trickled down my parted legs. I managed to look up, but was at once blinded by the white of the moon.

"I am in love," I said, though I do not know for sure if I was speaking aloud or not. "It is enough."

Thus began our future together, and I hoped it would last for as long as I lived.

Lightning Source UK Ltd.
Milton Keynes UK
UKOW042237171212

203800UK00002B/472/P